Reviews

"Ebony is an intriguing protagonist ... She is clever, resourceful, and strong, and it is easy to sympathise when her carefully guarded life is challenged"

- Rachel Churcher – author of the *Battle Ground* series and *Angels*

"A real page turner. I read it in forty-eight hours and struggled to put it down. That says it all!"

- Gybe Gilbert

"Immerse yourself in the lyrical world of the fae, dwellers, and shadows. A wonderful conclusion to the series that will keep you riveted and reading late into the night.

A thoroughly enjoyable adventure, with a heroine who doesn't always choose the right path, but perseveres regardless.

An adventure of hope and discovery you won't want to put down."

- Helen Garraway, USA Today bestselling author of the multi award-winning *Sentinal Series*

"M.J. Glenn's *The Dwelling Hunter* series is an action- and pathos-filled adventure, full of great characters, a well-realised world, and believable magic. *At the Door* is a fitting end to a corker of a trilogy."

- Deen Paulsson

Also written by M.J. Glenn

On the Edge (2020)

In the Dark (2022)

AT THE DOOR

FATE AND RUIN

The Dwelling Hunter Series

Book 3

M.J. Glenn

SB

SOFTWOOD BOOKS

SUFFOLK, UK

Published and Manufactured by Softwood Books
EU Responsible person: Maddy Glenn
Office 2, Wharfside House, Prentice Road, Stowmarket, Suffolk, IP14 1RD
www.softwoodbooks.com
hello@softwoodbooks.com

EU Rep:
Authorised Rep Compliance Ltd., Ground Floor, 71 Lower Baggot Street, Dublin, D02 P593, Ireland
www.arccompliance.com
info@arccompliance.com

Paperback ISBN: 978-1-0681509-1-3
Hardback ISBN: 978-1-0681509-2-0

For baby Leah, who taught me that writing with one hand while holding you with the other is the best way to work.

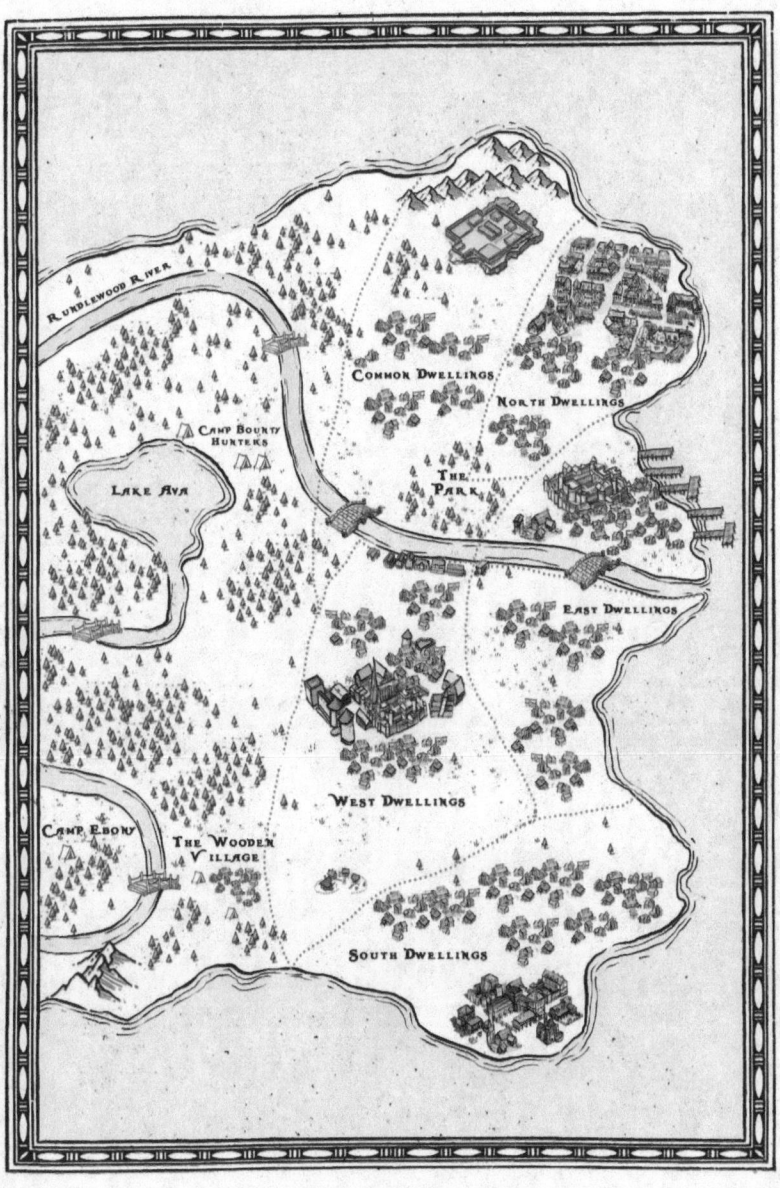

RUNDLEWOOD RIVER

CAMP BOUNTY HUNTERS

LAKE AVA

COMMON DWELLINGS

NORTH DWELLINGS

THE PARK

EAST DWELLINGS

CAMP EBONY

THE WOODEN VILLAGE

WEST DWELLINGS

SOUTH DWELLINGS

They say there's a Demon in the woods, lost to the darkness, cursed in the night. They say it has no thoughts, but thoughts are all it has.

It seeks a heart, a body of its own. To live. To breathe. To rule.

I know there's a Demon in the woods. I've seen it face to face. I've felt the chills of fear and grief that follow in its wake.

I know the way to vanquish, to make it meet its end:

Three must stand where the light is drawn, their powers intertwined and strong.

But beware the dark tide that spills through the gate, where shadows rage and burn.

To open and seal the tearing night, the —

1

Mary was being followed. A figure wearing a billowing red cloak. She brusquely walked down a thin alleyway, eyes darting from side to side. Her heeled boots echoed on the pavement as she veered towards the oil lamps lining the walls. She looked up and quickened her step, then stopped abruptly outside a large, red door. Taking two steps at a time, she pulled a large key from an inside pocket and fumbled at the lock, hands trembling. The door swung open, revealing a warmly lit, large entrance hall, a candlelit chandelier gracing the ceiling. It shut behind her with a thud. And Mary Donahue was gone.

"Find the Mother!" a whispered voice echoed. Images flashed by — so many scenes it was hard to keep track. Red eyes in the darkness, an archway, a blue ring, an old lady's kind smile, and then the light of the Fae, so bright it blinded. "Find the Sister!" the voice hissed.

Ebony lurched backward, one hand outstretched toward the vast yew tree towering before her. Her fingertips scraped against the bark — rough and ancient, with deep grooves like old scars — as she regained her footing. The touch left a smear of moss on her skin, damp and cold. The tree loomed silently above her, its twisted branches sprawling like arms in mid-reach, its roots breaking through the forest floor in thick, gnarled knots. Something pulsed just beneath the surface — not movement, exactly, but a thrum, faint and steady.

She stepped back, chest heaving, and stared up into its shadowed canopy. She had seen her aunt — Mary Donahue — by touching a tree. The tree that the Fae lived in.

She recalled trees racing past, branches whipping at her cheeks. Then her horse had bucked and she went flying forwards … he must have run off as she had fallen …

She was in the land of the Fae.

And the moment the FaeFolk had called her the 'Daughter of the Forest', the world had shifted. The name rang through her like the first birdsong at dawn. The yew tree — the magnificent home of the Fae — had beckoned her. Not with words, but with something deeper. A pull, magnetic and ancient. It had drawn her in and offered a vision of Mary Donahue. And now, in the corner of her eye, she noticed two archways — one a shimmering white, the other dark as midnight — and they wanted her. She could feel their pull. They pulsed with a quiet hunger.

She shivered. This was too much.

"W-what just happened?"

"Faelynn accepted you as one of its own," a voice said. Not a fairy's voice. It seemed almost wrong — out of place in this otherworld.

Ebony spun on her heel to find an elderly lady smiling at her, eyes so blue they sparkled, large, bushy white hair framing her kind, leathery face, ink stains on her hands. The picture of elegance, but at the same time wild and wise beyond her years, although Ebony couldn't quite place an age on her, as though time had stopped keeping count. There was something ethereal about her. Otherworldly.

"Hello, Ebony. It's so nice to meet you at last."

Ebony looked her up and down. Was she missing something? Was she supposed to know this person? The Fae seemed at ease, like nothing had changed. They flew about, not making a sound, going about their daily business, though Ebony could feel the watchful gaze of the Fae King. But she had the distinct feeling he was watching *her*, not this otherworldly woman.

"You don't know me," the woman said. "But I have known you a long time. Well, ever since you entered the woods."

"Who are you? How do you know my name?" Ebony took a step away from her and glanced at the Fae surrounding her. Would they protect her if this woman was dangerous? They had protected her before.

"I am the Sister. I have been watching over you."

"You — what?"

Ebony took a step back, her heel crunching a dry twig. The forest seemed to lean in around them, listening.

"You've been *watching* me?" Ebony narrowed her yellow eyes. "Why?"

"Haven't you ever wondered why the Fae adopted you? Protected you, shared their religion, ate alongside you?"

Ebony didn't answer. Her mouth felt dry.

"Haven't you wondered why they chose *you*," the Sister went on, softer now, "and no one else?"

Ebony's mind raced. Of course she'd wondered. A hundred times. But it was one thing to ask herself in silence — and another to hear it spoken aloud, like a truth she'd been avoiding.

"Well ... because ..." Ebony stumbled, "I respect them and their ways. I look after *them*, too."

"Yes, that is true. But they began protecting you the moment I discovered you. They look after you because I tell them to. The girl with the colour-changing eyes. You are unmistakably the Daughter of the Forest, just as your mother was."

"The *what*?" Ebony's voice cracked. "My *mother*?"

The woman nodded once, solemn. "She was the Daughter before you."

Ebony took an unsteady step back, her hands balled into fists. She shook her head, her eyes stubbornly remaining a curious yellow despite the fear bubbling up in her chest.

"This is just…" Her breath caught. "It's too much. No. I just—"

She broke off, turning away, blinking hard. The woodland around them swayed gently, but the world suddenly felt too still, like something was watching. Like everything she thought she knew had cracked at the edges.

She didn't speak. She glanced around instead, taking in the strange, glowing canopy before her, the soft silver moss beneath her boots. The Fae hadn't moved — dozens of them, standing on the branches like twinkling statues, watching her with unreadable expressions.

She lowered herself onto the grass beneath the towering

yew, the weight of everything crashing over her like a wave. She pressed her elbows to her knees, head in her hands.

Sam.

She could still hear his voice — his face haunted by the Shadow, cold and sharp. His eyes, once familiar, had turned glassy and strange. She recalled that presence, oppressive and heavy. And then that *thing* had reached for her — touched her.

'You are drawn to *me*, not Samuel Sanker,' it had said. 'You can save him if you come under my protection, under my wing.'

Every instinct in her told her not to believe it.

She'd called out. She wasn't sure how. Had she shouted out loud or just in her head? But somehow, the barn doors had flown open and she had run.

She had left him behind.

Her throat tightened. *Is he alive? Is he still in there?* The questions came like a sting.

No one spoke for a long moment. Only the wind shifted through the leaves, carrying scents of honey and wet stone.

"Just give her a moment," the Sister said softly.

But from the other side of the clearing, King Alvero

shifted. His wings rustled with quiet impatience. He said nothing, but his gaze was sharp, flicking between Ebony and the Sister.

Waiting.

Guilt made her stomach flip. She had run from her friends *again* and abandoned them to who knows what. The Shadow could have unleashed all hell on them.

And for the first time, it had touched her. She looked down at her arm, where she could still feel its cold grasp, and saw faint lines wrapped around her wrist, like an old scar from claw marks.

Why did the Shadow say she was drawn to it? Why had it been waiting for her? Yes, she had run from her friends again, but she had done it in self-defence. She'd had no *choice* but to run.

Just as she opened her mouth, the Fae spoke in chorus.

"Faelynn accepts you."

The words echoed through the clearing like a breeze through leaves — soft, but somehow final.

Ebony blinked, still seated beneath the yew. Her fingers pulled absently at a fraying thread on her sleeve.

"But… why?" she said, her voice quiet. "I'm not a fairy."

King Alvero flew onto the ground before her, his bare feet silent on the moss. His presence felt too large for the clearing, too large for his small size, as if the trees leaned away to make space for him.

"You are the Daughter of the Forest. One of the Three," King Alvero replied. "You have been sent to us to close the Shadow Door forever—"

"I wasn't *sent* to you—"

"It is fated. The prophecy says—"

"I fell off my horse and was thrown through a … some sort of archway?"

"She who can enter the Fae Door—" another Fae began.

"Stop." Ebony stood abruptly, brushing grass from her palms. Her voice trembled more than she wanted it to. "You keep saying things like this was all meant to happen. Like I was chosen. But I'm not—" She shook her head. "I'm not some kind of hero, fated to save you from the Shadowlands. I can't even protect myself from the Shadow!"

Her words hung heavy in the air, and the clearing fell quiet until the Sister sighed and spoke.

"Why do you think the Shadow comes for you?"

Ebony faltered, desperate for a quick retort. "B-because…"

She looked wildly around, as though the right answer might be growing in the grass. "It has a vendetta against my family?"

The Sister nodded. "Precisely."

Ebony blinked. Wait, what? She was right?

"The Shadows are kept in check by the Three," the Sister explained. "When they are united, the door can remain closed. But if the Three are lost … the door begins to crack. The Shadows gain power."

"But what does that have to do with *me*?"

"You come from a long line of Daughters of the Forest," the Sister continued gently. "The Shadow that escaped when the Mother was captured has made it his mission to destroy the Three and anyone standing in his way."

Ebony stared at her, her mouth slightly open, but no words came out.

It did make sense … it answered things she'd never been able to explain … and yet it made no sense at all.

"So … what now?" she asked finally, her voice barely above a whisper. "Why am I here?" Ebony asked.

"We will train you to defeat them."

2

"Defeat who?"

"The Shadows."

She blinked at him. "What — all of them?"

"The Wick," the king said, nodding at Ebony, "and her family will destroy the Shadows and close the door forever."

Ebony scoffed before she could stop herself. "But ... I have no family." That wasn't strictly true. She did have an aunt in the city.

"The Three are your family — the Sister, Daughter, and Mother. You will unite, and you shall triumph."

She looked at the woman with bushy white hair. She was part of her family? Surely not. She was too ... ethereal to be related to the scruffy teenager who lived in the woods.

Ebony shook her head, her eyebrows creased. "Hold on a minute." She rubbed her orange eyes with the heel of her palm. "Your prophecy says the Three will unite, destroy the Shadows, and close the Shadow Door?"

"Yes."

She folded her arms tightly across her chest and looked down at her boots. Moss clung to the worn leather. The weight of everything pressed against her.

"But the Mother is trapped in the Shadowlands."

King Alvero nodded sadly.

"So let me get this straight." Ebony raised a finger for each point: "We don't know how to open the door. We *also* don't know how to close it. We don't know how to find the Mother. And you want me to destroy the Shadows."

A pause.

"We have much work to do," Alvero said.

Ebony burst into nervous laughter and slowly shook her head. "It isn't possible."

"It is. So says the prophecy," the king said, as if this answered all of Ebony's questions.

A low murmur rang around them as the Fae all repeated, "So says the prophecy."

Without another word, Ebony strode away — away from the yew tree, from the Sister's ink-stained hands, from the eyes of the Fae who spoke in unison and made no sense at all. It was too much. Too loud in her head. It was all too much to fathom at once.

She didn't look back.

The stone ruins gave way to mossy ground beneath her boots, the remnants of crumbled walls now half-consumed by ivy and golden fern. She stepped through what had once been a doorway, its arch cracked and bowed with age, and passed beneath a row of empty windows that stared blindly at the sky. Fae symbols were carved into every stone brick — some neat and deliberate, others scrawled like warnings or prayers. Vines crept between the stones, weaving through the runes like veins.

A rusted iron gate, half-hinged and clinging to its post, marked the edge of the ruin. Beyond it, the land dipped into a gentle slope, where trees grew thicker and wilder with every step. The old abbey fell away behind her and the forest rose ahead.

The path to the trees wasn't really a path — more a meandering suggestion of where others might have walked before.

She found herself in the woodland of the Fae world; Fae symbols curled across the trunks of trees, etched in silver. The forest closed around her, cool and quiet and thick with green. Behind her, the last of the ruins sloped away.

There were no scurrying sounds, no nervous chirrups, no

crunching leaves. The woodland was a perfect green, not too hot, not rainy or windy. In fact, there wasn't even a breeze. The forest stood still, but not with trepidation. It was the stillness that comes with pure contentment. Pure peace.

Ebony pressed deeper into the trees, her arms folded tight across her chest. Her boots brushed through low-growing ferns and silver-blushed moss. She needed space. To think. To *breathe*.

So she walked.

If only I could do some hunting, she thought. *That always helps me clear my mind.*

Her foot caught on a root and she stumbled forward, catching herself with one hand against the rough bark of a low, twisted tree. As she straightened, something caught her eye — a pale shape nestled against the base of the trunk, half-covered by leaves.

A bow.

It leaned against the roots like it had been left there long ago, waiting to be remembered. It was elegant and strange, its wood smooth and bleached pale, carved with curling patterns that looked almost like writing. A quiver lay beside it, slim arrows fletched with silver-tipped feathers.

When she picked it up, her fingers closed around the leather grip as if it had been shaped for her hand alone.

She stood slowly, testing the weight. It was light. Balanced. Familiar.

A bird fluttered up from the branches, and Ebony took aim. Her jaw dropped as her one arrow pierced two birds in one shot. That had never happened to her before.

She collected the birds and held them by their talons over her shoulder. In the corner of her eye, she saw a squirrel scamper up a tree and, swivelling on her ankle, she took aim and loosed.

With a thud, the squirrel fell to the ground. Grinning, she collected her dinner. She would eat well tonight.

She turned to see a natural path to a small stream, trundling merrily through the trees. With a sigh, she eased off her shoes and carefully dipped her toes in the water. A perfect temperature.

Couldn't she stay in these woods forever? Food aplenty, warm sun, so many perfect places to camp …

She sighed. She had always wanted to know more about herself — her family, her eyes, her background. Here was the perfect opportunity to understand all that, but she was hiding — again. Hiding from the truth.

She set out her catches on the bank and splashed her face with cooling, fresh water. As she did so, she saw the shimmer of fish scales. With no other means to catch it, she instinctively reached in and, to her astonishment, caught the wriggling fish between her hands.

But how? How had she caught all of this with such ease? Something didn't feel right. It was too easy. She looked over her shoulder and through the eerily still trees.

She didn't need more food, anyway. She loosened her grip and the fish slipped out of her hands, continuing its journey down the steam like nothing had happened.

She sat down on the forest floor and tried to make sense of everything that had been said.

That woman was the Sister. As in, the Sister that the Fae prayed to in their many rituals. And they thought *she* — Ebony Wick — was the Daughter. Of the Forest. The Sister and Daughter of the Forest. It was madness. It had to be. She had often said the words — a sort of grace before eating a meal — but had she ever actually believed them?

"I thank the trees, the grass, the leaves. I thank the Mother, the Sister, the Daughter of the Forest," she mumbled.

It had felt good to have a ritual ...

The Mother had said the same thing. The woman in her dreams — the woman in the Shadowlands. She had called Ebony the Daughter of the Forest. But what did that mean? Who were the Mother, Sister, and Daughter?

She began to make a list of questions, then stood up, gathered her catches, and all too easily made her way out of the trees. The sun shone through the leaves, casting dappled shadows, and a natural path through the trees seemed to appear before her.

She emerged into the brilliant sun, the breeze playing with her hair.

She found her way back to the yew tree, where the Sister sat waiting on a large stone that had once belonged to a building. The Fae all seemed to have gone about their day, no longer a throng of sparkling eyes staring at her ominously, expectantly. The woman smiled as if Ebony hadn't stormed off like a petulant child, and waited for her to speak.

"Who are the Mother, Sister, and Daughter?" Ebony asked.

"Sit down and I will explain."

Ebony sat down on a large piece of stone, she supposed part of the ruins of the Abbey. She was perched so close to the Sister, their shoulders were almost touching.

"There were once three women from the same family, each with considerable powers — some called them witches, prophets, seers, shamans. Together, they could create something from nothing. They were feared throughout the land, as were the Fae. Magic has never been accepted by those who do not have it. After much persecution, the women and the Fae joined forces and created a land of peace and prosperity — Faelynn, where we are now." She gestured around them — an idyllic meadow marked by the ruins of something long lost. "They built a magnificent castle, surrounded by endless forest, and gave the Fae a safe place to live. They created their own children — cherubic creatures that grew into angelic, powerful beings. They became Gods to the Fae.

"But nature demands balance. Only some of their children gained powers — always at different times in their lives, but always the same pattern. A mother, a daughter, and a sister. Each of the three women had their own power. The Mother could speak to the dead, so she built an abbey where she practiced her abilities. The Sister could see the future, so she built an observatory in the tallest tower to watch the stars. And the Daughter could stir the hearts of others, transforming their emotions with a mere touch. But in a land of perfect peace and prosperity, these abilities weren't needed all too often and fell into disuse. As generations lived and died, their powers began to diminish.

"Eventually, they could no longer create their own children. They would have to come out of hiding and reopen the Fae Door. They would have to re-enter the world that had shunned them and create children without magic. The moment this happened, darkness began to seep in. Nature requires a balance. With such perfect peace came unfathomable darkness. A black door appeared in Faelynn, leading to the realm of Shadows. Lost souls. The ghosts of the dead that have never found peace. They began to seep out, one by one, causing fear, sickness, death, destruction. Back then, the door was wide open — and some of the children found themselves pulled in, never to return.

"The Mother wanted to close it, but the Sister and Daughter said it was too dangerous. In the dead of night, the Mother walked through the Shadow Door, believing she could close it and still return. Well ... she's still in there." The Sister sighed.

"We believe the Shadows fed off her soul while she was in there, and before she could close the door, they flooded Faelynn with their darkness, tearing it asunder. The palace was shredded like paper — you see its ruins here. Rubble.

"The Mother of the time could speak to the Shadows, and we believe she coaxed them back into the Shadowlands, but she was taken with them. Trapped. The Sister and Daughter fled Faelynn and have lived amongst the people ever since. They could always be distinguished because, outside Faelynn, the Daughter's eyes would change colour with her emotions — the only remaining evidence of her power — and the Sister ... well, her powers of perception get less and less perceptive by the day." The Sister frowned, and Ebony could tell she was speaking from experience.

"There has not been another Mother — she is still trapped. But the dynasties of Sister and Daughter have been passed down. To you and me."

Ebony sat quietly, taking it all in, then asked, "So ... are we sisters?"

"No, not quite. Over time, the generations have got a bit muddled. But we are related somehow."

"So ... my mother was the Daughter before me?"

"Yes, and she had the same colour-changing eyes. If you had grown up knowing her, she would have told you all of this — your lineage. I expect your father didn't know."

Ebony had often been able pinpoint her exact emotions

— in a way that others didn't seem able. But she couldn't quite understand this new feeling. It some ways, everything the Sister had said made sense, while in others it seemed like a fairytale that belonged to someone else. But if she really thought about it ... something clicked inside her. Like a box had been ticked. A long-hidden question had been answered about who she was. It made sense somehow. She was the Daughter, and this woman was the Sister.

"So ... so if we're the Daughter and Sister of the Forest ... what does that mean? Why does it matter?"

"The Shadows are returning."

Ebony shivered.

"Yes, you've felt them too. Perhaps even seen them."

"There's more than one?" Ebony's eyes would have turned red ... yet she could tell they remained a stubborn yellow.

"Currently, there's only one loose beyond the Shadowlands. But there are thousands. And they are only too ready to destroy our world. It is up to us — the Mother, the Sister, and the Daughter — to stop the Shadow Door from opening once more. We must close it. Only ... we don't know how. The Shadow Door appeared so many centuries ago, the secrets have been lost with the Mother."

"They didn't write them down anywhere?"

"No. And even if they did, you wouldn't be able to read them, would you?"

Ebony blushed.

"There is no shame in it."

Ebony fell silent. Shouldn't she have more questions? Why was she accepting this information so readily? It just felt ... right. It all made sense. It clicked into place like a puzzle that was almost finished.

"What's your name?" Ebony asked.

"In Faelynn, I am just the Sister, and you are just the Daughter."

3

"Explain to me again why I need to learn all of this?" Ebony huffed. She was sitting cross-legged on the cold flagstones of what had once been the abbey's chapter house, tall cobblestone walls etched with a thousand symbols surrounding her. Some were shallow and neat, others deeper, ragged, as if carved in a hurry or anger. The roof was long gone; only the star-pinned sky arched overhead. In the centre of the old room, opposite Ebony, sat the Sister, tending to a small fire. Her serene face showed not the slightest hint of impatience.

Ebony's gaze drifted over the symbols, the lines and curves strangely familiar. "How will I know which ones to use?" she asked, quieter now.

"You'll learn them as you go," the Sister replied. "For now, use the simplest: symbols for courage, for sight, for strength of mind. Of course, the symbol for 'open', a line through a cross, will be the most important to learn — but you won't need it until—"

"Until I actually go through the Shadow Door."

The Sister frowned and nodded.

Ebony traced one of the symbols into the dirt beside her boot with a hesitant finger: three horizontal lines. The stone felt warm, as if it remembered being touched before. *Strength of mind.* What good was that against those shadowed claws and burning eyes?

She forced a thin smile, pretending she understood. The Sister had that calm, unshakeable air that whispered: *Trust me. I know what I'm doing.*

The fire cracked softly between them. The walls threw back the flickering light, making the symbols seem to shift and ripple like water.

Finally, the Sister spoke again. "Tomorrow, you must enter the Shadow realm to look for the Mother."

Ebony stiffened. "No." The word came out too quickly, raw in her throat. "I'm not going back there. Faelynn gives me peace — no darkness, no burning cities. Please don't make me go back there."

"But we need to know what the Mother did all those years ago, and it seems you are the only person who can go there."

"How did you know that? I didn't tell you about my dreams …"

"I am the Sister, am I not? I have perception and foresight," she replied, tapping her forehead. "Things come to me in cryptic ways ... but they all seem to make sense in the end."

"How do you know I'll even dream about the Shadowlands? I haven't seen them once since coming here."

"We have our ways ..."

"What ways?"

"We can induce certain types of sleep—"

"What? How?"

"We can discuss that later. What matters is that you find the Mother and discover what she did all those years ago. We need to garner her knowledge of the Shadows and their realm."

Ebony huffed, her eyes a bright red.

"We can tether you to this plain and wake you in case things get ..."

"Out of hand," Ebony finished for her. She didn't want to think what 'out of hand' might comprise of.

"For now, we must sleep peacefully. I shall see you tomorrow."

They put their fire out and parted ways. The Sister liked

to sleep in the cloisters, where there was a ceiling, but Ebony had adopted what had once been the infirmary. She strode across the field, the grass damp with dew, and settled herself on a straw bed, gazing up at the stars of Faelynn.

The sun rose, a startling orange, mist lifting off the fields. Ebony could swear she'd seen a deer frolicking through the long grasses by the trees the day before. Or had it been a week ago? Time worked differently here, she was sure of it. But she hadn't found one bit of evidence to show that deer lived in Faelynn's forest.

The burning orange sky slowly turned to blue as Ebony wandered through the strange trees. In Rundlewood Forest, she had learned to clamber through the undergrowth, race and duck through spindly trees — all without making a sound. It had made her feel alive, the world whipping past in a blur.

But Faelynn's forest was different. The woodland seemed to part before her. It saw her coming and made way. Berries, wild garlic, herbs, and fruit trees made themselves known, like they were begging to be picked, always ripe.

She could always hear a trickling stream and had whiled away many hours in them, barefoot — none of the stones would hurt her feet, they were so perfectly round and smooth. And the stream held her upright.

She emerged from the tree line into a large open field. Before her stood four looming, crumbling buildings — the ruins of the castle — and the most magnificent tree in all of Atlaan. If they *were* in Atlaan, of course. The Fae realm was separate from the world of the Dwellers and Humans, visible only to those who could pass through the Fae Door.

In the far corner of the field stood two archways, or doors, a few metres apart. One was pure white and decorated with carved symbols. The steps leading up to it were made from, and lined with, white crystals. This was the Fae Door — the door she had accidentally entered. It led back to the world of the Dwellings, where Ebony was no longer safe. The other door was identical, except it was black as night. A large semi-circle which almost seemed to breathe by itself. Its stone was beautiful, though cracked and decaying. This door was altogether different, and Ebony didn't like to remind herself of where it led.

Ebony breathed in the delicious smell of grass and wildflowers. She was safe here. She always had enough food, she was protected by the Fae, she was respected — almost unnervingly so — and best of all, there was no—

No.

She mustn't think about it. She was safe. Life was good. She would not let the past ruin her peace. She took a deep breath to steady her beating heart. A smile spread across her face, her eyes a warm hazel.

A magpie flew past Ebony's ear, dipping and diving until it reached the tallest point on the tallest wall and surveyed its kingdom.

As she walked towards the cloisters, she admired the thousands of Fae symbols carved into the stone. Every surface was etched. She had only ever learned a few Fae symbols — how would she ever learn all of these?

By the great Fae tree, the little creatures seemed to be engaged with one of their morning rituals, flying in dizzying circles round and round the trunk.

Ebony ran her hand along the walls of the abbey, taking note of some of the more simple symbols that she might be able to recreate.

"Ah, Ebony, good," a voice said.

How did the Sister always seem to know where she was?

"The Fae are ready for you now. It is time."

Ebony's heart sank. She knew exactly what that meant. It

was time to enter that dark dreamworld again, surrounded by deadly shadows, but this time somehow have total autonomy and uncover long-forgotten secrets from a woman who had been missing for hundreds of years. No pressure.

She followed the Sister through the cloisters of the ancient abbey, her footsteps echoing off the stone walls. They entered a dimly lit chamber, one of the only ones remaining that still had a roof, its air thick with the scent of various herbs and flowers. In the centre of the room, a circle of Fae stood waiting, their natural light shining.

At the centre of the circle was a bed made of woven vines and soft moss, surrounded by bundles of herbs tied with delicate silver threads. The Fae nodded to Ebony as she approached, their eyes reflecting centuries of wisdom and mystery.

"Lie down, Ebony," the Sister instructed softly. "Remember, you are searching for the Mother. She may hold the knowledge we need to defeat the shadows."

Ebony nodded, swallowing her fear as she lay down on the mossy bed. The Fae began to chant softly, their voices weaving a melodic spell that filled the room with a calming energy. The Sister placed a wreath of lavender and chamomile around Ebony's head, its scent immediately relaxing her tense muscles.

"Put aside all emotion, all fear. Empty your mind. Don't let them feed off you. Keep focused on the task at hand."

Ebony wanted to respond with, 'How am I supposed to do all of that?', but she felt so heavy she couldn't seem to move her mouth, let alone make a noise.

"Breathe deeply," the Sister whispered, holding a small vial under Ebony's nose. "It's just a scented oil," she reassured her. "It will help you enter the dream state."

Ebony wasn't sure she needed help. The smells of the room were heavy enough as it was, lulling her senses and quietening her thoughts.

She inhaled the fragrant oil, her eyelids growing heavy. The last thing she saw before her eyes closed was the serene face of the Sister and the glowing forms of the Fae.

Ebony found herself standing in a dense, dark forest, the trees twisted and gnarled, their branches reaching out like skeletal hands. The air was thick with mist, and shadows flitted at the edge of her vision. She took a deep breath, the scent of lavender still lingering in her nostrils, grounding her.

Ebony began to walk, her senses alert. The forest seemed to shift around her, the shadows moving closer whenever her focus wavered. She could feel their malevolent intent, a coldness that seeped into her bones. But she pressed on, determined to find the Mother.

After what felt like hours, she reached a clearing and saw an all-too-familiar sight: a burning city of ash and thick grey smoke. It was like the world was in black and white, all colour diminished. The buildings were crumbling, their skeletal remains silhouetted against the destruction. Shadows moved through the streets, their shapes flickering like colourless flames.

She moved cautiously, her eyes scanning the ruins for any sign of the Mother. The air was filled with the acrid scent of smoke and whispers in her ear, words that she couldn't make out.

Out of the corner of her eye, she spotted a flash of colour — blonde hair disappearing round a corner.

"Come back!" she called, but her voice sounded like she was underwater.

Ebony startled awake, the Sister's expectant gaze weighing on her.

"Well?"

"I saw her—"

The Sister gasped and beamed. "What did she say?"

"Nothing. She didn't stick around long enough for me to even say hello."

The Sister nodded like she'd expected that response. "We'll try again tomorrow."

And they did. For multiple days in a row, Ebony was sent back to the darkness of the Shadow realm, desperately seeking the Mother, but she was always distant, always turning away, her pale hair catching the dull light before she slipped into shadow.

On her fourth attempt, frustration rose and she yelled at the Mother's retreating form, *"So that's it? You won't help?"*

The Mother halted and looked like she might actually respond, but by the time Ebony reached her, she had turned away, her gaze lost in the drifting ash, then as quick as a flash she disappeared out of sight.

But Ebony had got somewhere at last. She had made the Mother stop and think.

When she awoke, she shook her head at the Sister again, heaved herself up from the dusty floor, and sloped out into the trees.

4

Dappled sunlight shone through every branch, animals offering themselves up as prey. Every day was perfect blue and sunshine, a light breeze playing with her hair.

She wanted for nothing. And it was maddening.

All her life, she'd fought for what she needed — learned skills to survive, fine-tuned her 'I don't need your help' expression. She only now realised how much she enjoyed the thrill of the hunt. The uncertainty, the relief, the adrenaline, the need. But Faelynn gave her everything on a plate.

She knew she should feel grateful — many people could only dream of this sort of luxury. A ruined abbey, always in sun, all the food you could want. There was no sickness in Faelynn.

But what was the use of a girl like Ebony when nothing and nobody was needed? Well, one thing was needed — but the Fae were asking the impossible.

The only real purpose Ebony had now was to find the various plants the Fae used in their rituals. And there were a *LOT* of rituals.

She strode out of the forest, an exit opening before her, of course, and the tall grasses leaned away from each other, creating a meandering path. She was sorely tempted to tread through the long grass, but every time she tried, a new path would instantly form.

Before her stood the impressive ruins of the Mother's abbey at the centre of a lush green field of daisies. The walls were a mixture of cobblestones and limestone; sturdy, an impression on the landscape.

It was days before the Sister managed to coax her into trying again, and Ebony only agreed to it through sheer boredom. If Faelynn was a utopia, then utopias were boring, she decided. No challenge, no excitement, every day exactly the same. She had to keep reminding herself to be grateful that she was safe. And even though she was going to the Shadowlands every day, the shadows paid her no mind, almost like they were used to her being there. That didn't stop her fear of them, though. She knew what they were capable of.

Massacre. Fire. Torture. Possession.

She could never grow complacent in the Shadowlands.

She let the Sister's herbs lull her to sleep for the umpteenth time and fell back into the world of shadow and ruin.

The world around her dissolved into smoke and darkness. The air turned cold, heavy with ash that clung to her skin like damp cloth. Before her, crumbling towers rose against a bruised sky. Shadows drifted through the ruins, restless and silent, their shapes wavering like dying flames.

Ebony pulled her cloak tighter around her shoulders, forcing her legs to move, each step crunching over ash. Somewhere in this dying city, the Mother was hiding.

Ebony caught sight of a figure standing alone beside a shattered archway. The woman didn't move, didn't even seem to breathe — just stared out over the burnt city, her face silhouetted in the darkness. Heart pounding, she stepped closer, boots sinking into black dust.

But yet again, the Mother fled, gliding away from her down a blackened alleyway, disappearing behind a crumbling house.

Ebony rounded the corner, and before her stood a figure emerging from the smoke, her form shrouded in a tattered cloak. She moved with a grace that seemed out of place in the destruction around her, while all around them, the world was falling apart, burning like old parchment.

"So you'll just let them win?" Ebony called after her. "You'll let them destroy everything, and you'll let me fail, too? Is that what you did last time — turn your back and hide?"

For a moment, the ash seemed to freeze mid-air. The Mother stopped.

Slowly, she turned.

Perhaps it was the bite in Ebony's words or the echo of old guilt buried under centuries of ash — but this time, the Mother stopped.

The figure lowered her hood, revealing a face etched with lines of age and grief, yet her eyes sparkled with a fierce determination.

Ebony took a deep breath, steadying herself. "The shadows are growing stronger, and we need to know how to close the Shadow Door. The Sister told me you hold the knowledge we need."

The Mother tilted her head, pale eyes catching the dim, ashen light. "You found the Sister?"

"Well ... I suppose you could say she found me."

The Mother's gaze flickered away. "Then you know enough."

"No, I don't," Ebony pressed. "They said you know how to close it."

The Mother's jaw tightened. "Closing it is not the same as stopping it from breaking open again."

"Then tell me what is," Ebony demanded.

For a heartbeat, the Mother's face almost softened — regret, guilt, something unspoken. "Child," she whispered, "I did what I thought would save us. And still it cracks."

"Just tell me — what do I have to do?" Ebony sighed with exasperation. "How do we defeat the Shadows? How do we close the door?"

The Mother tilted her head slightly, as though listening to something far away. "Even if I told you, it would change nothing," she whispered.

"What do you mean? It would change everything."

The Mother finally looked back at her, and for a heartbeat, Ebony glimpsed something ancient and tired behind those pale eyes. "This place must fall," she whispered.

Ebony swallowed hard. "How?"

The Mother's expression flattened into something distant, unreachable, and she shrugged.

Ebony raised her eyebrows. If the Mother was shrugging, then they truly were in trouble. She didn't take the Mother to be a shrugging type. She was a deity of sorts, so graceful, so sure. How could she not know what to do?

Ebony stood there, the silence pressing against her like cold stone, realising that whatever help she had hoped to find from her wasn't coming.

"Follow me."

The Mother moved at such a speed, gliding through the streets like she was half-shadow herself, and Ebony had to run to keep up.

High on a hill above the burning city stood a blackened archway, shrouded in flickering darkness.

"All those years ago, I battled my way up there, fought off the darkness, and kept to my purpose. Today, they fiercely protect the door ... we cannot go there now."

"But what did you do when you reached the door?"

"Talismans, symbols, herbs ... scattered around in a Faery ring. But they wear off over time if they are not strong enough. The strongest talisman I ever made didn't make it in with me ... a blue ring ..."

"Do — do you mean this?" Ebony held out her hand and showed the Mother the blue ring that now never left her finger.

The Mother's face changed, her brow furrowed, her features sharp, her eyes dark. "Why did you bring that here? You are not ready to wield it!"

Ebony took a few steps back, her heart racing.

"If they take it from you ..." the Mother whispered, a voice like ice. "That could be the end of us all."

She held up the palm of her hand and thrust it towards Ebony. An invisible forcefield threw her backwards, and somehow she was back in the trees, surrounded by red eyes and flickering, shadowy shapes.

Darkness descended, shadowy claws tearing at her skin. She screamed out for help, and the world began to spin. Was she underwater? Which way was up?

Stop! Please stop! *she cried out in her mind. And the world fell still. All she could feel was her heart thumping.*

It took a few minutes for the pain to kick in. Stinging all down her arms, like lacerations had been torn into her skin. She sat up and opened her shining red eyes, shaking from head to toe. She was in the abbey, the Sister trying to soothe her, Fae all around her, glowing with anticipation.

"You're safe now, Daughter. You're safe."

Ebony tore off her shirt, revealing red welts covering her arms. The Sister gaped and traced one of the wounds with her finger. Ebony winced.

"What happened?" she whispered.

"They attacked me."

"They aren't supposed to touch you ... when in the dream

state, you're not really there. How … how did this happen?"

"I don't know!" Tears threatened to well up in Ebony's eyes.

"What did you see, Daughter? The Mother of the Forest?" King Alvero asked.

"Are you serious?" Ebony spat. "All you care about is the Mother … but your Daughter of the Forest is here suffering, right now, because you keep forcing her into that place."

"We didn't anticipate this …" the Sister responded hesitantly.

"And here I thought you had the ability of foresight?"

"It comes and goes …"

"Well bring it back again. But I am *not* going back in there willingly. To hell with the Mother. She was useless, anyway."

Ebony tried to stand up, but her legs were still shaking.

"So you did see her?" the Sister asked.

Ebony turned her most fearsome look of disgust on the Sister and spat, "Yes, I saw her. I spoke to her. She closed the gate last time with your talismans and symbols, but she got herself trapped in the meantime. She has no answers for us … only to *not* do what she did."

Ebony wondered what it must be like to live in that place all day every day, and her anger deflated. The Mother had endured it for hundreds of years.

She let out a sob and covered her face with her hands. There was no way she would be able to do all of this alone. But who did she have? A mysterious woman only known as the Sister, and the cryptic Fae. They didn't care for her beyond achieving their prophecy.

With all the strength left in her, she heaved herself to her feet and strode into the forest, ready to chop something, shoot something, rage at the brambles, get lost in the trees and never return.

But while she was used to battling the undergrowth, enjoying the catharsis that came with it, in these woods it was like the trees cleared a way for her. She *couldn't* stray off the path. She *couldn't* get lost.

It felt wrong. Unnatural.

She stopped short and yelled at the trees, screamed out her fears, her confusion, her anger, ready to hear the birds clear the rooftops with a flurry. But nothing moved.

It was like the forest was smiling at her — a benign, childlike smile — and nothing she did would mar its peace.

Shouldn't she relish this? Didn't all people endlessly seek peace and happiness? Yet here it was in all its perfect glory ... and it felt dead. Lifeless.

5

Images raced by. A world of Shadows. A woman with glistening blue eyes. A black mirror — rippling, enticing ... no, it was an archway made of black rock — black as night. The steps that led up to it were lined by sharp, black, shiny crystals. She longed to touch them, but something told her to stay away. She gazed into the rippling surface inside the archway — like the ripple of waves at night. Her arm reached out ... what would the ripples feel like against her fingers? She took a step forward ...

Ebony bolted upright, her heart hammering in her chest. She checked her hand — the blue ring was still there; she checked under her straw pillow — her dagger was still in place; she glanced to her left — her boots were untouched. Her new bow and quiver leaned against the wall to her right, patiently waiting for her. These were her worldly goods now. Everything else had been left behind.

Just another one of those dreams. I'm safe, I'm safe, she reminded herself.

She stretched and yawned, then climbed out of her hessian blanket, which had become tangled around her legs, as usual. She shook it out and made her bed, next to the old cobblestone wall of the ruined abbey that was now her home. Pulling on her boots, she slipped her dagger into its normal hiding spot beside her ankle and gazed up at the sky. Blue. It was always blue in Faelynn.

Surrounding her bed were four crumbling stone walls, remnants of the Mother's abbey from times past.

There used to be an entire castle with a dormitory, a grand library, and an infirmary. The balneary, refectory, and cloisters still stood, but the other chambers had been reduced to rubble when the Mother had been pulled into the Shadow realm. Faelynn had relied on the strength of the Three, which was lost when the Mother was taken, or so the Sister had said.

Ebony peered through the archway into the field beyond before striding into the never-ending forest.

An arrow whistled through the dappled light of the trees and, with a thud, hit its mark. The bullseye of a target she had drawn onto one of many trees. She had grown tired of catching animals; they were always too ready to be caught. They might as well wander up to her feet and walk into a net or skewer themselves over a bonfire.

The sky was a perfect blue, not cloud in sight — the same as every day in the fairy realm. Ebony missed the sight of clouds and the smell of a damp forest after rain. On her other shoulder she held a sack full of greenery — edible leaves, medicinal sap, dark purple berries for painting symbols, and little wild strawberries that the Fae would happily feast on. They were preparing for the Summer Solstice, a celebration of growth and prosperity. Ebony wondered how they knew which season they were in, or even what day it was, when every day was perfectly blue and hot.

Leaving the woods behind, she strode into the closest building, the only one that still had a roof. The walls were pockmarked with missing bricks, Fae sitting in the gaps, dangling their legs over the side. The room was alive with activity as the Fae prepared for the evening's feast.

Striding through the swarm of fairies, who expertly avoided her, she headed to the back of the cavernous room, where the food was being stored in barrels. The first time Ebony had seen their food stores she had begrudged them. Why hadn't they shared this with her during those winters when she had been starving and alone in Rundlewood Forest? But she soon realised that it was all poisonous to her. The Fae could eat hemlock and nightshade, though they also loved strawberries.

"You're almost late," a voice said into her ear. The Sister.

"Which means I'm on time," she replied, emptying her sack into different barrels.

"You must get ready for the ceremony."

"Stop fussing, I'll be there."

"In your robes?"

"Of course."

When the Fae had realised she would join them for the Summer Solstice, they had immediately gone to work making a suitable gown for her. They hadn't been able to do the entire ceremony since they had lost the Mother to the Shadowlands, but they'd made do with just the Sister for years, so having the Daughter with them was a bonus. Ebony had been assured she would only be required to speak some words. The rest of the ceremony remained a mystery to her.

A red fairy named Ozmiah, or Oz for short, perched on her shoulder, admiring her finds. He was no bigger than a hummingbird, with gleaming wings like a dragonfly's, and his wide, bright eyes seemed almost too large for his delicate face.

The Sister peered over her shoulder. "Good, we need more dye to draw our symbols."

"Isn't this enough? How many symbols do the Fae need to draw on us?"

"*All* of the symbols is customary. But this should be enough dye."

Ebony gulped. She had seen the walls of the abbey festooned with different symbols.

A group of Fae flew across the room to collect the berries she had amassed, then pulped them to get their juice. It would stain her skin for days, but she didn't mind. Only the Fae would see it anyway.

"I need to wash and change. I'll see you there."

"Of course."

Ebony left the room through an archway into the cloisters that led to the baths, a room full of steaming water that never seemed to get cold. Today, the baths were blissfully empty and quiet. The first time she had used them had felt odd — bathing in hot water? She had grown used to the cold river water. But she now relished the heat as she slipped in, her dark hair pooling around her.

The baths were wide enough to swim across. She smiled as she floated on her back, imagining herself peacefully drifting down her old stretch of river. But she could never go there again. Sam knew where it was, therefore the Shadow knew as well. What had become of Sam since she'd left? *Fled*. The last time he'd lost her, the Shadow had tormented him. She shouldn't have left. She shouldn't have—

No.

She wouldn't think about those times or those people. Things had changed now. She was the safest she had ever been. This was true peace, and nothing would take it away from her, however frustrating it could be sometimes. She dunked her head underwater and let the heat wash away her dark thoughts.

When she emerged from the water, she noticed that someone had delivered her robes to her and taken her clothes away. Probably Oz. He had been put in charge of taking care of the Daughter during the time of the celebration, which essentially meant ensuring she was always in the right place at the right time. He took this role very seriously but found her very hard to control.

She rolled her eyes as she dried off. Her robes consisted of a long patchwork dress, decorated with ivy and white flowers. They'd clearly salvaged whatever materials they could. It fell to her feet and left her arms bare. She carefully slipped it on before fastening the green ceremonial cloak around her shoulders.

Running her fingers through her thick hair, she tidied it as best as she could before plaiting it down her back as she always did. She then left the baths and headed to her new den, where she could see her dirty clothes piled neatly by her bed. As she walked through the archway into her ruin, she was surrounded by buzzing fairies.

"Hey, what's going on?" They flew on her shoulders and into her hair. "I just did my hair!"

Oz hovered before her. "Almost the spitting image."

"Spitting image of who?"

"The Daughter. The first Daughter of the Forest. This was her dress."

A shiver raced up her spine. They were treating her like some kind of deity. Fairies began tugging at her hair, delicately undoing its knots, pulling it into a tight bun, and braiding it intricately around her forehead. Lastly, a crown of daisies was woven into her hair. The fairies retreated and admired her.

"You are ready. It is time," Oz announced. He beckoned her to follow him. He himself was wearing green robes, a bone staff in his hand. The sky had begun to darken as Ebony followed him across the field towards a ball of light.

"You look magnificent," the Sister said as she appeared beside Ebony, resplendent in her own gown of gold, her curly hair plaited tightly against her head.

Ebony smiled. "Um, so do you."

"Do you remember your lessons?"

Ebony rolled her eyes. For a week, the Sister had been teaching her the history of each Fae tradition — in particular the meaning of the Summer Solstice. "Yes, I haven't forgotten."

"This ceremony helps us keep the Shadow Door shut. You must say the words exactly right and believe them fully in your heart. Though I know you do. You have diligently followed the Fae beliefs for years."

Ebony stopped walking and softly touched the Sister's arm. "I'm ready. I know what to do." She gave her a reassuring smile.

"I know. You have found true peace here."

Ebony wasn't sure how she felt about that. She smiled and continued walking across the meadow. She wasn't sure of a lot of things in this realm, only that she was safe. Its sole purpose was to be a safe haven, after all.

A pull from across the field held her attention. Her gaze turned to that mysterious archway … beautiful and dark. It wanted her, and it knew she was curious.

She shook her head and approached the grand tree, and the sea of Faelights parted to reveal the king and queen, standing on a magnificent branch adorned with carved symbols.

"Behold, the Daughter of the Forest," King Alvero declared. The swarm began to buzz but fell silent as Queen Coralia raised her hand.

"It is an honour, Daughter, to have another one of the Three amongst us once again. We can only pray that you will all be united once more."

"Let us begin," King Alvero said.

The Faelights moved to make a perfect fairy ring around the tree as an old, wizened fairy emerged from a hollow to stand beside the king and queen. Eldria was gold — the oldest fairy alive. She still clearly remembered the Mother and the words she used to say.

"Sister, Daughter, repeat after me," Eldria said. The two women nodded. "Mother, Sister, Daughter of the Forest," Eldria began in her crackling voice. "Protectors of the realm of the Fae. Light of life, peace in the darkness. Three may make a crowd, but together we are one. Never touched by darkness, ever strong, a lasting hope. Mother bring us peace, Sister bring us plenty, Daughter bring us light."

A deep knot had settled in Ebony's stomach. Why hadn't they told her the words before she had agreed to this? They promised so much. A lot of it she couldn't deliver. She glanced at the Sister, her mind tumbling with nerves. She nodded at Ebony with an encouraging smile on her kind face and repeated the words with confidence.

"Mother, Sister, Daughter of the Forest," Ebony began. "P-protectors of the realm of Fae and beyond."

Did they really think *she* could protect them? She could hardly protect herself!

"Light of life, peace in the darkness ..."

She'd certainly *felt* lighter and more peaceful than ever before, but she was sure she'd never *brought* light or peace to anyone else. She only ever brought fire and fear.

"Three may make a crowd, but together we are one."

She hardly even knew The Mother — she'd met her properly only once, and that had been in a dream. How could she be one with The Mother, a woman she hardly knew, and the Sister, a woman she had only just met?

Then came the hardest line to say out loud. She took a deep breath and prayed that the Fae couldn't see the lie on her face.

"N-never touched by darkness? Umm, ever strong, a lasting hope." Her words echoed across the field. She couldn't do this. She couldn't declare such bold statements about herself. Not when they were outright lies. She swallowed heavily.

"Mother bring us hope. Sister bring us plenty. Daughter bring us … light."

Red eyes flashed through her mind, the image of a shadowed claw on her wrist. The cuts she had woken up with after her last foray into the Shadowlands had mostly healed, but they stung in a flash of pain, and she yelped.

She stumbled back but caught herself before she fell.

"Are you well, Daughter?" the queen asked.

"Y-yes, I just …" The entire Fae race was hanging on her every word, the Sister staring at her, confusion in her eyes. "I, umm, saw a vision of the Mother."

Another lie. But she couldn't tell them the truth. She *had* been touched by darkness. Did that mean she was no longer the Daughter?

"What did you see? Did she say anything?" Eldria asked, her expression more energised than Ebony had seen it in these past weeks. They had all blindly bought her lie.

"Umm, she said her words. Mother bring us peace."

"It is a sign. She accepts you as one of us, one of the Three. Let us rejoice!" Eldria cried out.

The circle of light began to rise and flew as a ball toward Ebony and the Sister. Fairies clung to them wherever they could, creating beacons of light, warm against their skin.

A group of Fae, including Ozmiah, the king, and queen, flew above Ebony's head, and as the tips of their staffs touched, a bolt of lightning shot up into the sky, so bright it was blinding. They repeated this above the Sister. Ebony shielded her eyes and felt water drop onto her hands. The heavens opened and rain poured from the sky, soaking her to the skin; 'purifying' her, they explained.

The Sister clutched at Ebony's hand and beamed. The Fae urged them both towards the dry hall, where they were surrounded by flaming torches on the walls, casting tall shadows. With the flame's warmth, they were soon dry. A large bowl of red liquid was flown over to Ebony and the Sister, and the same Fae that had plaited their hair began drawing symbols on their skin — every patch of skin they could touch — her arms, feet, legs, ankles, cheeks, eyelids, lips, ears — everywhere. The liquid was cold at first but soon dried, dying their skin a dark red.

As the Fae flew back to admire their work, the kind declared, "Let the festivities begin!"

The rain outside stopped, and the Fae rushed back outside, twinkling, like a thousand stars racing across a dark sky. The Sister strode outside with them, disappearing into the darkness of the night. For a brief moment, Ebony was left alone as each fairy attended to their duties — delivering, serving, and sharing the food. A large bonfire was lit, and Ebony was soon led to a tree stump so covered in moss it was like sitting on a pillow. Before her stood a large stone table — the old altar, she presumed — and on it was a feast of fruit and vegetables. Some Fae joined her, eating and chatting merrily on the slab of stone, while the rest perched in nearby trees or on smaller stones, detritus from the ruins, or flitted about in a frenzy of joy. The Sister sat on the other side of the bonfire with the king and queen.

After the feast came the dancing. A large bonfire was lit, and the Fae frolicked through the air, an image of glee as they twirled, dipped, and dived. Ebony spun and spun with the Sister until she was dizzy and giddy, but the Fae begged for more. It was late when she finally stumbled into her bed of moss, her hair still adorned with flowers, her skin dyed red.

Sinking into her soft bed of moss, she fell into sleep with

a peaceful smile on her face, her robes splayed across her like a protective blanket. She hardly considered what the next day might bring.

6

The moon was always full in Faelynn, a land that seemed trapped in one everlasting summer's day. A light breeze rustled through the Fae Tree. The abbey was silent but held the distinct energy of an after-party, and the cracking of glass echoed through the night.

Ebony woke with a start. Had she dreamt it? Imagined it? She was sure she'd heard something smash. She opened her eyes and slowly sat upright. Through the archway leading out of her chamber of the abbey, she could see a few small lights floating across the field. What was going on? The Fae were never up late at night. They feared the dark.

She stretched and clambered to her feet, realising she was still in her ceremonial robes. Not wanting to dampen them in the tall grass, she quickly changed into her dark outfit that she had intended to wash — black trousers, black tunic, her old jacket, her dagger in her boot. She could feel her mask in her pocket, but she didn't need it now. From her archway, she watched more Faelights float across the field to the far corner.

Her stomach twisted. That was where the Shadow Door was.

Ebony waded through the long grass to join the growing throng of Fae. The trees glistened and hummed, and two Fae hovered before the Shadow Door, the Sister standing beside them, also still in her ceremonial gown. Ebony had never dared stand so close to the door before. She could see its black surface shimmering like silvery waves. It was mesmerising to watch.

Not sure if she was meant to see this, she peered from behind a tree, trying to discern what the Fae were saying. She recognised their voices. Ozmiah, the king and queen, and a few of their closest advisers.

"Daughter, we know you are there," the Sister declared.

Tentatively, Ebony stepped out from her behind the tree and smiled apologetically. "What's going on?"

"Come. See for yourself."

Her heart beat faster the closer she got to the door — the entrance to the Shadowlands, where the Mother was trapped.

"Look at the surface. What do you see?" the Sister asked.

"It shimmers — it moves. Like a mirror made of silvery water." Ebony's heart grew still and calm, her body light as she watched the door's patterns.

"Look closer."

She could feel the pull — a desire to step through it and enter the world beyond. If she looked any longer, she might actually give in. But as her eyes became accustomed to its patterns, she began to see it emerge: a jagged line ran down the mirror, from tip to toe.

She felt dizzy, light-headed. It was as if her body had been unmoored, drifting like a feather on a rising breeze. The world around her seemed to stretch and thin; the air itself felt different, thick with the smell of acrid smoke.

A collective gasp sounded around her, and she could hear distant voices calling. A sharp pain stung her fingers, but dissipated so quickly she hardly noticed it at all. She looked down at her hands, or was she looking at the forest floor? Her palms were no longer solid — she could almost see through them. Should she be frightened? She could hardly feel a thing anymore. She stared at her hands, her feet, her arms, all less solid than they were only minutes ago. They looked almost shadowy.

She looked like *the* Shadow, her fingers tendrils of smoke.

She stumbled back — and then she could feel the pain. A hundred tiny jolts from every direction. The Fae were shocking her with their lightning staffs.

"Hey! Hey, stop!"

She had found her voice again. Her hands — they were solid, and her feet felt heavy. She breathed a sigh of relief. That was a close one. The door had almost sucked her in.

"You must leave. Immediately."

Ebony searched the darkness for the voice — the king's voice. He was perched on a branch nearby, bone staff at the ready. Ebony began to feel red welts swelling all over her body. How had she not felt their shocks? She had seen grown men die from such an attack.

The king's words finally came to her. "I— what?"

"You have touched darkness. You must leave."

Ebony looked away. "I don't know what you're talking about. I've never touched the darkness." Not a lie, really — the darkness had touched *her*.

"The words you spoke last night were no game, Ebony Wick," the Sister snapped. "You spoke untruth, and now the door has cracked. It is opening once more. No human ... no *creature* of this land would fade to shadow like you just did unless they had been touched by darkness."

"You lied to the Fae, Ebony Wick," the king added, "And now you must leave."

"I didn't lie! Nobody asked me what had happened —

why I found this place. You all just assumed I am some god-like work of perfection. I didn't even know the words I had to say until it was too late."

"It is never too late to speak the truth," the Sister snapped.

"You caused this," King Alvero said, gesturing to the Shadow Door.

"Ebony." The Sister's face was stern. "Your presence here is a danger to all of us. You must leave. Now."

Ebony rubbed at the stringing welts on her arms and legs. She couldn't quite believe what she was hearing. They surely didn't mean it?

"Sister — what's going on?" she asked, her voice cracking.

"You spoke falsehoods in a sacred ceremony. I warned you. Those words have kept the door shut for hundreds of years, but with your falseness ... you have brought darkness to Faelynn."

"What? No! No, I didn't. I didn't mean to ..." *Why do I always have to ruin everything?* "I called for the Mother's aid to escape the Shadow, and she led me to you. I'm supposed to be here, protected and safe. I'm — I'm the Daughter. One of the Three. I can't leave. It will — it will find me."

"You will not lead the Shadow into Faelynn. You must

find a way to remove its mark if you wish to come here again," the Sister said.

Ebony's hands shook as tears sprung to her eyes. A wall of Fae lights gathered before her, bone staffs pointed her way. Shaking, she raised her arms in surrender and backed away across the field. The Fae flew in a dizzying circle around her, forcing her towards the Fae Door.

"Please, don't do this. Don't send me away. I'm safe here. I have looked after you as you have protected me. I forgave you for killing my friends — I am the Daughter!" Her eyes blurred, tears dripping down her cheeks. "P-please," her voice cracked.

They were nearing the door now, shimmering with a white light, a crystal archway etched with Fae symbols.

"Don't make me leave. It will find me — kill me. Take me ..."

She didn't actually know what it would do if it caught her. She had never stopped to consider what it actually wanted from her. She had never given herself the chance to find out.

The Sister grabbed her arm and stared intently into her eyes. "You *must* remove the Shadow's mark if we are to keep the door closed. But you cannot stay here."

Ebony began to violently shake, tears streaming now, her eyes flicking between so many colours — shades of red, black, and brown. The Fae came together in one large ball of light and touched the tips of their staffs. She stared, wide-eyed. She had seen this last night. A blast of energy surged forth into her chest, and she stumbled backwards through the Fae Door, just as she had once stumbled forwards into Faelynn.

The world fell silent. She was in a wood, a crystal archway before her. She wiped her eyes to clear her vision and stepped through the Fae Door. But she did not emerge in Faelynn. She was still surrounded by trees, not an abbey in sight.

"No." She tried again and again, to no avail. In the distance, an owl hooted.

It was night time in Rundlewood Forest, and darkness pressed in around her. Ebony crouched by the base of the archway and held her knees close to her chest. The Fae were just trying to teach her a lesson — about honesty, perhaps. They were training her for something. They would let her come back in the morning.

The air felt cold. Was that her fear? Was it winter in The Dwellings? How long had she actually been in Faelynn? Or perhaps it just felt cold compared to the beautifully warm nights in the Fae realm.

She shivered and hugged her knees tighter. She doubted sleep would come so easily out here. Every noise made her flinch, her red eyes darting about. These woods weren't a haven of peace. She could hear it; feel it. Fear.

Eventually, sleep took her, and she dreamed of crumbling bridges and ash falling from the sky. And red eyes staring at her from the darkness.

7

It was still dark when she awoke. Her body was stiff and creaked as she tried to move, her muscles tight. She heaved her cold limbs to her feet and inspected the Fae Door, her eyes growing accustomed to the darkness. It looked exactly the same this side of it, except it was surrounded by trees, no meadow in sight, and a dense ring of small mushrooms circled the crystal archway. Ebony strode through the door, hoping against hope that she would find herself back in that field.

Nothing happened.

"Sister?" she called. "Queen Coralia? King Alvero? Please let me in."

Silence.

In the dirt before the archway, with her index finger, she drew the symbol for welcoming spirits and tried walking through again. But still the woodland stayed the same. Her heart lurched in her chest and she collapsed to the ground again. She belonged nowhere. She had nowhere to go. Nowhere was safe. The forest was haunted by the Shadow, Faelynn had banished her, and the city was riddled with gangs. And it was all her fault. She had unleashed all of this.

She began to shake and curled up into a tight ball, lying down in the dirt. She didn't care when a sharp twig snagged at her hair and lefts wisps trailing in the muddy soil.

Fear clung to her like a second skin — the memory of the warm safety of Faelynn and the shock of its loss pressing down on her chest. But lying here, trembling, would do nothing. She sucked in a breath, steadying herself.

She stared into the trees, expecting danger to come leaping out at any moment. A bird flew from a tree, and she flinched, inching herself closer to the safety of the Fae Door. What had happened to her? She had once been so fearless. Now, fear gnawed at the edges of her thoughts, and here she was, a shivering wreck. But she would not let fear root itself. The peace of Faelynn had pampered her, softened her resolve. It was time to take stock of her situation and work out what to do.

As her eyes grew used to the darkness, she began to make out the shape of a figure through the trees. Was she imagining it? Her pulse began to race, but she stayed still, afraid to announce her presence.

The figure's head turned, and two red eyes shone like flames.

She was on her feet in a heartbeat, fear racing through

her, and her legs took her; she hardly cared where, just *away*. Whether she was going mad or not, she needed to move. She crashed through the darkness, branches whipping her arms and face, pulling at her hair. Her cold muscles called for her to halt, but her instinct screamed at her to run.

RUN FOR YOUR LIFE.

Two pairs of bright red eyes. Two figures racing through Rundlewood Forest. One crashing her way through, startling every living creature in her path, the other silent as death.

Ebony's throat burned, raw with every ragged gasp. Each breath rasped like hot iron scraping her lungs, her chest aching with the effort. She stumbled, her vision swimming with black spots, but forced her legs to keep moving. The air felt too thick to swallow, every breath a battle. She wanted nothing more than to stop, to double over and heave air into her starved lungs — but the instinct to run, to flee, was stronger than the pain.

Where would she go?

She risked a glance behind her — it was still there, following like they were attached by a rope. She stumbled and tripped headfirst into a large tree, its rough bark tearing at the skin on her forehead. She yelped and felt blood on her fingers. But that didn't matter now. She had to keep going. But where?

At that moment, the heavens opened and the sky roared. Thunder rolled through her chest, as rain hammered down in sheets, cold and relentless, soaking her in moments. Her hair clung to her face in thick, dripping strands, mingling with the warm, sticky blood on her skin. Each breath tasted of wet earth and iron. Her clothes hung heavy, plastered to her body and pulling at her shoulders with every stumbling step. Water streamed into her eyes, turning the world into shifting shapes and shadows. She wiped them with a trembling hand, blinking against the blur, willing her legs to keep moving. But her muscles burned, lungs tearing, and she knew — she couldn't keep this up much longer.

Another glance behind her. The rain hardly seemed to affect the shadowy figure, those red eyes set on its purpose. It was gaining on her but she couldn't run any faster. A sob left her throat and she tumbled to the ground. With dread, she watched the figure draw closer — a shape stitched from darkness itself, shadowy tendrils licking and curling around the trees like living flame.

"What do you want?" she rasped.

It towered above her, a living night. Instinct took over — she raised her hand to shield her face, fingers trembling as she pressed her palm against her brow. The cool band of her blue ring dug into her skin. This was the end. The Shadow had won.

Then, light flared.

From the blue stone on her ring, a sudden, searing glow burst forth — cold and brilliant, cutting through the storm and the darkness alike.

The light glowed through the trees, making the raindrops gleam like falling shards of glass.

The air was filled with a high-pitched shriek, like nails on a chalkboard. It rang through her ears and pierced her frightened soul.

She looked up as the Shadow recoiled, its swirling tendrils writhing violently, before it turned and fled into the night, dissolving among the trees.

Her breath clouded in the rain-chilled air, her heart thundering with questions she couldn't answer.

The darkest being to ever exist had fled from *her*. But why? How had her ring lit up like that? Was it because she was the Daughter? It had never done that before. She lowered her hand slowly, her chest heaving, staring at the faint, dying glow of the ring.

The rain continued to fall, blending with the tears on her

face. Her chest heaved as she sobbed, and her body shook. Relief. Terror. Exhaustion. Shock. Confusion. She cried for it all.

The rain slowly died down as morning light reached through the canopy above. Ebony shivered uncontrollably — with cold, with fear, with exhaustion. She had seen her death — expected it. Felt that sigh of surrender. She had accepted her fate. Yet somehow she had escaped it.

She had to find somewhere safe. She couldn't go back to Faelynn, that much was clear. She had no way of contacting the Fae. And she doubted she would ever find the Fae Door again without a guide. Was she still in Rundlewood Forest? She hardly knew which way was up.

There was one place she could try. It would be dangerous ... but she needed to collect a few things from her den first, if it was still there. She used a nearby branch to pull her aching body to her feet. *Not again*, it cried. No, she wouldn't run. She didn't even know which direction to turn. But at least she had a plan.

Glimpsing the autumn sun through the trees and trusting her instincts, she chose a direction through the leafy forest and hoped she was heading the right way. Had it really been a year since she'd met Hunter? Her dysfunctional, deluded uncle. It had been early autumn when he'd broken into her camp. From the look of the trees around her, it seemed autumn was in full bloom, the trees a brilliant orange, the forest floor a blanket of leaves, acorns, and conkers.

Out of habit, she collected conkers and sweet chestnuts as she walked, filling her pockets. She used to feed the conkers to the Fae, a delicacy to them, and sit by the fire peeling and crunching on sweet chestnuts. They were good when roasted, too.

She eventually started recognising the trees — *her* trees — dappled sunlight making patterns on the forest floor. Not the oppressive darkness of wherever she had just come from. She knew where to go now. With purpose in her stride, she quickened her pace and even began to jog, a sense of relief and possibly even joy filling her tired heart, her eyes turning a hazel-gold with anticipation.

There it was — the river; the remnants of her old den; the tree she had tied her uncle to. She gazed at last year's camp, memories of a more simple time playing out in her mind's eye. Hunter. The Fae. Her spoils. Buried under a nearby tree was a small stash of coins for emergencies.

She dropped to her knees beside the old oak, the ground cold and slick with rain. With numb, mud-slicked fingers, she scraped away wet earth and rotting leaves, nails biting into the soil. The smell of damp roots and moss filled her nose. At last, her fingers struck cloth — a small, sodden bag. She tugged it free, mud clinging to the coarse fabric, and cradled it in her palm.

With a heavy sigh, she continued on her way. She knew where she needed to go now. To the south, towards the Wooden Village. It didn't take long to find it; she knew this part of the woods so well.

She could see life from within — activity in the central square, carts coming and going. They seemed to be doing well, her absence hardly noticed.

She skirted around the village, careful not to be seen. Only once did someone see her — a face she didn't recognise — and she did her best to look like she was supposed to be there. And why shouldn't she be there? She could feel a strange pull, like her heart was tied to an invisible string, pulling her home.

With sheer willpower, she remained hidden, and eventually her den came into view. Untouched. Like she'd never left. The last time she had been there, Sam had been so sweet to her. She'd felt safe, wanted, accepted. But had that been him or his … alter ego playing with her? Unconsciously, she placed a hand over her heart as if holding in a ball of pain that was all too ready to topple out. She blinked away tears, shivering in the biting autumn air, and took a deep breath, stepping into her camp.

Inside her den it was like time had stopped. Nothing had changed. She found the bow and arrows Sam had given her, gathered up her blanket, and piled the rest of her belongings into her old sack, careful not to make a sound.

She decided to leave her bivouac. If she took it down, it would be too obvious that she had returned. It was safer for those in the village to think she was never coming back — or dead. She didn't want them looking for her and risking their lives and her safety. If the Shadow thought they knew anything about her whereabouts … she daren't consider how strong it had got, feeding off Sam's tortured energy.

That pull was there again, tighter than before. Surely just one look in wouldn't harm anyone? She would make sure she wasn't seen. She crossed the small wooden bridge, her sack slung over her right shoulder, and hid behind the first wooden shack she reached. She jumped and stifled a yelp as a door slammed shut only a few feet away. She felt the force of it on the walls she was leaning against.

"You know he doesn't mean it, Anna," came a kind voice that Ebony recognised. Jaymes.

How is Galen? she wondered.

"He's so stubborn," Anna replied with a huff. "Sam used to be only too ready to start a rebellion."

Ebony's stomach lurched at the mention of his name, but she ignored the sick feeling in her throat and strained her ears to hear what they were saying.

Anna continued, "Now he's telling us to sit tight and do nothing while our village and rights are controlled by the bloody Jades? Well, I won't."

Of course — how could Ebony have been so oblivious and self-centred? She had feared that Sam might have been broken by the stress of losing her — by the torture the Shadow had inflicted on him as a result. But in truth, his greatest problem was the Black Jades. He was probably hardly thinking about Ebony at all.

"There will be logic behind his reasoning …" Jaymes said, though not very convincingly.

"Maybe there is. But he's not making it clear enough. And anyway, there is no leader of The Foryx. I can do what I want."

"Don't do anything stupid, Anna."

"Well, thanks a lot for your faith in me."

"No, I didn't mean it like—"

The pair fell silent, and a chill raced up Ebony's arm.

"It's back," Jaymes breathed.

The birds fell silent, and the wind stopped rustling the trees. The world felt still and cold, like death.

"Leave," said a chilling voice. The voice of Ebony's nightmares. The voice that had screamed at her through the trees. An unearthly sound like chipped ice.

Ebony's heart thumped so loud she was worried she'd be found out. She had been so stupid to go back. The Shadow was showing itself in the light of day now — claiming its ground, its power. And Anna was worried about the Black Jades?

She couldn't go back to the Wooden Village, that was for sure. And there was no way she'd be living alone in the forest anymore. Not with the Shadow intent on— she daren't finish that sentence. The city was riddled with gangs, most notably the Black Jades — a criminal organisation that hated her more than the Snatchers had.

There was only one place she could go. It was probably a long shot, but she might as well try.

8

On the front doorstep of a townhouse in the South Dwellings, a dirty bundle of clothes had been dumped. It was a large pile — quite out of place in the lavish front garden. The rain had left a puddle on the path that led up to the stone pillars, stopping at the steps leading to a tall black door.

The door opened, and a shriek could be heard all down the street. A tall woman in a bright blue corset and a white skirt stared dumbfounded at the pile of rags that had been so rudely deposited on her doorstep. It was everything she wasn't. Hair pinned perfectly into place, diamond-crusted earrings, smooth, radiant skin, a little blue hat perched on her head. She was the picture of gentility and she knew it.

The rags shivered and moved. It *moved*. A small face surrounded by a mass of knotted black hair looked up at her — at least, she thought it was a face. It was covered in something red; even the eyes were dark red, almost black, and shining with helpless tears.

"M-Mary Donahue?" the rags muttered.

Wary that a Jade could be watching from the shadows, ready to make an example of anyone who looked vulnerable, she glanced up and down the street and, with tremendous effort, took the girl inside, closing the door behind them. The market could wait.

She stood at the edge of a splintered bridge, the boards beneath her feet covered with black ash. The air stank of smoke and salt; far below, the river twisted, thick as oil, swallowing the ruins that toppled into it.

Ahead, a tower loomed over her, its twisted turrets clawing at a sky. A corridor of archways stretched out before her, impossibly long, each arch darker than the last.

Two red eyes burned in the shifting dark, glaring through her, hollow and endless.

"Ebony Wick," the voice rasped. It scraped across her bones, coiling around her heart. "Come to me."

She took one step, then another, breath shallow, each footfall echoing through the hollow dark.

Then, all at once, the world lurched. The bridge cracked beneath her, splitting open, and the river below swallowed her scream.

And in the darkness, those red eyes.

Ebony's head spun and she hardly noticed her surroundings. She was so cold she didn't think she would ever feel warmth again. Something red flickered in her vision, and she flinched.

A voice reached her, calling her away from the ash and decay. "Shh, it's okay. You're safe now."

She was laid down on something soft and squishy, and a blanket was tucked around her.

"Sleep. You're safe now."

Was she dreaming? She must have been. Though she didn't often have dreams like this.

She was wearing some old, blue pyjamas that were far too big for her and she was tucked into a double bed covered by two blankets, one of them adorned with lurid green flowers. Before her was a large, white fireplace, the tail end of a fire sizzling behind an ornate grate. The walls were lined with yellow wallpaper, and a painting hung of an over-sized horse. There was one window, but only a chandelier giving light. A chandelier?

In one corner of the room was a wooden table, with a silver platter holding jugs and glasses that looked like they'd been made out of ice. Next to the table was chair with a pile of her clothes — dirty, torn rags. Underneath the chair were her boots. She hoped her dagger was still tucked inside one of them. Propped in the corner rested her bow and the worn quiver of arrows Sam had given her, the fletchings bent from days of rain and travel. A rough old sack slumped beside it, its seams frayed from years of use. Folded at the foot of the bed lay her thin blanket, still smelling faintly of smoke and the forest.

These were her worldly possessions.

Where was she? Maybe she'd gone mad at last?

The events of the previous day slowly filled her mind. She had battled through the forest and stuck to the shadows in town, terrified that any passing glance might belong to a Jade. She had promised them inside information about the Bounty Hunters once — and then vanished before she could deliver. And she knew this would have angered them. They already hated her as it was.

As she'd crept along the narrow lanes, she'd glimpsed them at work: a pair of men she recognised from the Jades' ranks — one with a jagged scar over his brow, the other twirling a wicked-looking knife. They had cornered a ragged boy, shoving him to the cobbles and kicking him when he didn't answer their questions fast enough. The scarred man pressed his blade to the boy's cheek, his mouth twisted in a grin Ebony knew all too well.

She'd turned away before they saw her looking and dragged her weary body further into The Dwellings until she'd reached a street she recognised. She had seen it in a dream once.

With her last ounce of strength, she'd approached a door and hoped beyond hope it was the right one. But by that point, even three steps had been a challenge. One moment she'd been at the bottom of them, the next moment she was sprawled out by the front door, having tripped, and the world went dark.

And now she was here, in a vast house in the Southern Dwellings with a beautiful wolf-skin blanket on top of a blindingly green duvet.

She tried to move, but the room began to spin and her head throbbed. Something wasn't right.

She had felt this once before. That creeping, sinking heaviness. Cold seeped into her bones. Her limbs felt like stone, every breath an effort. Exhaustion swallowed her thoughts, leaving only fragments behind — flashes of light, the scrape of a door, a voice she couldn't quite catch.

Time slipped away from her, dissolving into a fog of aching limbs and half-formed memories. Was it night or day? How long had she been here? She couldn't tell. She was so tired — so terribly tired — and the world kept drifting further from her grasp.

Days passed in a blur. Or was it weeks? Ebony wasn't sure. It felt like a lifetime. The room had been foreign once — a lavishly decorated double bedroom with more comfort than Ebony could have ever imagined. But after some time, Ebony already felt at home in it. When she couldn't stop shivering, the room had piles of blankets ready for her. When she was so thirsty she couldn't speak, water appeared at her lips. When her forehead throbbed with heat, a cold cloth calmed her. When the world spun and her thoughts jumbled together, someone was always there to stroke her hair and soothe her to sleep. Sometimes she was sure it was her mother by her side, dressed in a silk gown the colour of pale rose, fine lace at the collar and cuffs. Her dark hair was swept up and pinned with a small, gleaming comb.

Ebony ate little and drank a lot — though she didn't get much choice over *what* she drank. Some of it was hot, some cold, and some of it tasted disgusting. Her bones ached and her she coughed and coughed, her chest burning, but being awake with her mother by her side — or whoever it was — was heaven compared to being asleep.

She knew it wasn't *actually* her mother — just Mary's maids nursing her back to health — but it felt good to pretend.

Dark towers loomed before her, grey ash falling from a dark sky like snow. Before her stretched a burning city, shadows aimlessly roaming the decaying streets. She was the onlooker, but there was an odd pull, a drive, a need to join them. She was sure she was there for a reason. She needed something — someone. But what was it?

A vision of a willowy blonde lady filled her mind, only to be replaced seconds later by those red eyes.

Piercing. Hungry. Desperate.

Curls of smoke formed long, sharp fingers as they reached out to touch her arm — claws burrowing into her flesh as blackened blood seeped out, and she became one of them — tendrils for fingers, her body not fully there.

"You're mine," said a cold, chilling voice, and she realised it was her own.

A cold as chilling and harsh as ice filled her lungs as she gasped for air, her throat pierced by a thousand icicles—

"Ebony! Ebony, wake up! Shh, you're safe now." Her mother's voice. It had to be.

She blinked awake. The world was blank. White. Not the darkness of her dreams. She heard a fire crackle, and her beating heart quietened. She was in her camp. No. She was with Sam. No, that wasn't possible. She was with her aunt. She had an aunt — Mary Donahue. An aunt who actually seemed to care about her.

A warmth spread through her heart as she looked up into Mary's caring eyes. How long would this one last? How long until the Shadow took her too? Her eyes grew glassy and she blinked away tears.

Mary wiped Ebony's hot forehead with a cold cloth and stroked her hair, damp with feverish sweat.

"It's okay, I'm here. You're safe."

"Thank you," Ebony croaked.

9

Mary had often taken in the lost, the unwanted, the uncared for. She would train them up in some job or other and get them back on their feet. But her work was cut out with this one.

A criminal urchin outlaw with magic eyes who was currently riddled with fever and covered in burns.

The girl was refusing to eat. She couldn't get a doctor; she couldn't risk anyone outside the house finding out about the fugitive that was her niece. The Black Jades would hang her for hiding magic from them. She already had enough to hide as it was … but she would make room for this one somehow. And perhaps telling her staff the truth was the best option. Well, most of the truth.

Ebony lay in a confused stupor for a whole week. Her eyes flickered between colours so fast, Mary couldn't keep track. Was that normal or should she be worried? She didn't recall her sister's eyes changing so fast. Red, purple, blue, hazel, gold, grey, turquoise, black, brown, amber, crimson — a cascade of colour moving so quickly, they almost blended into one.

When Ebony's eyes began to settle into a steady lavender, Mary felt she could breathe easy. Ebony's pulse grew calmer, her body more still. She stopped muttering in her sleep. She would be okay, Mary reassured herself.

She headed downstairs for dinner — her staff had started asking questions about the strange girl in the spare bedroom.

One thing she knew for sure. Ebony couldn't leave this house without protection. What would the neighbours say if they saw her eyes? 'Dark magic in the Donahue household.'

But Mary had seen dark magic, and Ebony wasn't it, however haunted she seemed.

"Oh good, you're awake," a voice said, and a door closed. Ebony tried to sit up, but fell back into the cushions.

"Stay there, my dear. You need to rest." The woman approached and began fussing with her blanket, tucking it around Ebony's body.

"Wh-what's wrong with me?" Her voice felt like gravel and it hurt to swallow.

"You have a fever." The woman didn't mention the strange burn marks all over Ebony's skin, but she must have noticed them.

Ebony's heart sank. A girl she had once known in The Clink had died of the fever. She had tried so hard to escape the Shadow, yet would she now die of a sickness? Ebony's eyes turned from stormy grey to red.

"Not to worry. We'll have it cleared up in a few days. You came to the right place."

"I ... er ... I came to find you ..." she croaked, trying to recall the events that had got her here.

"I know you did. It was only a matter of time. I know who you are, Ebony Wick. I've been looking for you for a long time. I'm Mary Donahue."

A memory surfaced. She had once robbed the Donahues and tied them to a tree. Was she now a captive? Was her aunt going to hand her over to the Jades as retribution? Her eyes a bright red, she bolted to her feet, but instantly regretted it.

"Oh, my dear, I didn't mean to scare you. Don't worry about the past. All is forgiven."

"But, I—"

"You robbed us and left us to die."

"Well ... yeah."

"And you changed my life forever. You gave me purpose. In fact, being robbed by the Demon in the Woods worked wonders for my social standing!" Mary laughed. "*Our* social standing, I should say," she added as an afterthought, referring to her husband.

Ebony sat down slowly, a quizzical and wary look on her sickly face.

"How do you even know who I am without my mask on? When I turned up at your door, I could have been any old beggar …"

"You're Ebony Wick, Demon of the Woods." Mary gave her a coy expression and a playful smirk.

"But— but do you know who I *really* am?"

Mary Donahue smiled — a warm, inviting, trustworthy smile. It wrinkled her eyes and made them sparkle. "I have never known anyone but my sister to have those eyes. You are my long-lost niece."

Mary touched Ebony's forehead with the back of her hand and grimaced. "Now then, I think it's about time you had a warm bath." Ebony gave her a look of incredulity and gratitude and tried to stand up again. "It's okay, dear. I can carry you."

With surprising strength, Mary scooped up the bag of bones that was her niece and took one step at a time through a bright corridor and into the largest bathroom Ebony had ever seen. The bath was steaming and felt like heaven as Mary carefully lowered Ebony into it, night clothes included.

She carefully peeled the clothes off the girl's body and piled them behind her. Ebony's skin was an odd shade of red, which seemed to bleed off her in the water. She had welts covering her body and a large gash across her scalp, which Mary only found after washing all the dried blood out of her hair. The girl's true face was visible at last, and Mary's heart skipped a beat. She could see her sister in those features. Her sister with those colour-changing eyes that everybody feared; the same hair, the same high cheekbones. There was less of the girl's father. Only if you looked closely would you see Mary's brother-in-law.

She delicately wiped away the blood and grime as Ebony sank into the blissful heat.

"Isn't there anyone else in this house?" Ebony asked, noticing the eerie silence.

"It's late, everyone is sleeping. I'm sure you will meet the staff tomorrow."

Ebony's eyes widened. She couldn't risk strangers telling the Jades where she was.

"Don't worry, we're all friends here. This is the safest place for you to be."

Nowhere is the safest place for me.

"No one knows I'm here?"

"Currently, not a soul."

"What about … things without souls …"

Mary shivered. She had a feeling she knew what Ebony meant. "I have seen no signs of souls or not-souls. Nobody knows you are here. Unless you wish me to get a message to someone?"

Ebony thought for a moment. Was Hunter even still alive? "No, don't tell anyone I'm here."

"My staff will find out eventually. Likely by tomorrow morning. But," Mary held out her hand to stop Ebony's retort, "we are not friends to the Jades, here. We look after our own. And they don't have to know your background or anything you don't want them to know."

"So what will we tell them?"

"We will tell them you are my niece, which is the truth."

They fell silent as Mary thoroughly washed Ebony's dark hair, filled with grime and forest.

"You're not scared of me?" Ebony stated.

"Why would I be? My sister was just the same. Just as wild when she wanted to be. And she, too, had those eyes."

Ebony stared at her, disbelievingly. "Why are you helping me?" she asked, playing with the water on her fingertips. "You must know what happened to them. My parents."

Mary paused. Should she tell the full truth? Perhaps not just yet. She would wait till the fever had passed. "These are dangerous times," she said. "An orphan on the street is not safe. But you are so much more than just an urchin … I have wondered sometimes where you might be, whether you were still in the Dwellings. I saw you in town sometimes. But then you disappeared for almost a year."

She had been gone almost a year? No, she had been hiding in the Wooden Village for a long time.

"I was … away," Ebony replied.

Mary could tell she was holding something back, but let it slide. She suspected there would be a lot about this girl that would remain a secret.

"But it won't be easy hiding my existence all the time … I can't stay in here forever. But I can't— I can't go out there, either."

"The Jades are looking for you."

"Yes." Red eyes. Dark shadows. "Yes, that's what I'm worried about," she lied. The Shadow could be lingering on Mary's doorstep, biding its time. Was it too much of a risk to stay here? The Shadow hadn't entered yet, so maybe it was safe? "Does your husband ... Lord Donahue ... does he know I'm here?"

"Oh, he's fine with it."

Ebony creased her brow. *That wasn't actually what I asked ...*

When Mary was satisfied that Ebony was clean, she heaved her out of the bath and wrapped her in a towel, then carried her shivering body back to her room.

"I'll bring you some clean night clothes," she said as she tucked the girl into the blanket again. Ebony's eyes drooped and she was quickly asleep.

10

A few days had passed in a blur, and Ebony lurched awake as she heard voices outside her bedroom door, her eyes yellow. Whispered bickering it sounded like.

She raised her shaky head and chanced a glimpse out of the room's only window. The sun shone brilliantly through a gap in the curtains. One of those cold, crisp mornings, though winter hadn't fully settled in yet. Though it could have been afternoon for all she knew.

With a sigh of relief, she fell back against the pillow. It didn't like the sunlight. It wouldn't hunt her in the daytime. She hoped.

Her head was less foggy today, forming full thoughts. *I didn't realise the Donahues were* this *rich*.

She was lying on what felt like a cloud in the largest four-poster bed she'd ever seen. The room was wood-panelled, the walls adorned with paintings of important people — she assumed they were important.

"But how do you know that she's safe? You remember what she did to you?"

A woman's voice. One of the maids, she supposed. She spoke with an accent more commonly heard in the East Dwellings.

The voices outside her door were rising in pitch and she could hear their every word.

"Of course I do. But she's family, and she probably had no choice back then. Poor girl has been living in the woods alone for years!"

So she knew *exactly* who Ebony was. But how?

"We need to be careful with this one, my lady. I know you like to take in your waifs and strays, but this is different."

"How so?"

"Things have changed! The gangs on the streets … if they find out—"

"They won't."

Ebony's stomach churned with guilt. She was the *reason* those gangs ruled the streets.

"But they might! If they see her—"

"They *won't* see her."

"Her eyes, my lady. How will you hide her … her *magic* from the other staff. If they tell the Jades—"

"All of our staff are steadfastly loyal to House Donahue. I have given them a job and a home, and they know that full well. Now, that young girl in there is my niece, and I will do everything in my power to keep her safe, and there is nothing you can do about it. Unless you intend to go to the Jades yourself?"

Ebony's eyes widened and shone with distinctive flecks of gold. She'd never had anyone stand up for her like that before.

"My lady, you know I would never do such a thing. I only pray that we all stay safe."

The pair fell silent, and Ebony heard the tap-tapping of her newfound aunt's shoes approaching her door. She lay back on her pillows, feigning sleep.

The door creaked open.

"My dear? Time to wake up." Mary approached her bedside, and Ebony blinked and stretched as if she'd only just awoken.

"How do you feel today?"

"Umm ... better, I think."

"You look better," Mary said with a kind smile. "Now that you're on the mend, I'd like to talk to you about a few things ..."

Her thoughts drifted, her eyes wandering to the window.

She went to open the curtains, and Ebony shielded her eyes from the light.

"But first, let's get you cleaned up and fed. Do you think you're ready for food?" she asked, placing the back of her hand on Ebony's forehead. "Yes, much better," she murmured. "What do you like to eat for breakfast?"

"Uhh, I don't really have food in the mornings ..." Ebony couldn't recall the last time she'd had breakfast. Back in the clink, maybe? But that could hardly be considered *food*. "Besides, I've outstayed my welcome already ..."

"Nonsense! Am I correct in saying you have nowhere else to go?"

Ebony nodded and gave her an apologetic look, her eyes now a brilliant sea-blue.

Her aunt sighed. "I figured as much. Not to worry — this is what I do. I take in waifs and strays."

"Which am I? A waif or a stray?"

"My dear, I think you are something entirely different." She gave a kind smile that made Ebony's chest feel warm. "Now then," Mary began with a frown. "You are my niece. You are my family. And as a member of my family, you shall share in my house accordingly. You are to be treated in all respects as a Donahue. And in this household, we take care of each other and we eat breakfast, lunch, *and* dinner when we are well enough to do so."

Ebony smiled, or was it a grimace? Was she expected to behave like a lady as well as be treated like one? She couldn't think of anything more embarrassing.

Mary gave her a sweet smile and then said something Ebony would spend the next week puzzling over before deciding that perhaps her aunt was just a bit eccentric and this had to be accepted as the norm.

"Domus mea est domus tua."

With that, Mary pulled a red cord that hung beside Ebony's bed and activated some kind of bell deep within the house. Out of nowhere came scurrying a petite blonde girl with nervous eyes.

"Daisy, my niece has come to stay with us. Ebony Donahue. As you may have noticed, she arrived rather unwell, but the fever has passed now. So, to business. Could you please draw her a bath and then show her to the dining room for breakfast?"

"Yes, my lady," Daisy replied with a curtsy.

"Good. See to it, then." The girl scurried out of the room. "I shall see you downstairs, dear."

Ebony was left alone again for a few minutes until Daisy arrived holding a pile of logs and a basket of twigs. She was so wafer thin, Ebony worried she might break under the weight.

"Here, let me," Ebony offered, jumping out of bed, then instantly regretting it as her head swam.

"Are you okay, ma'am?"

"Yes. Yes, I'm fine." Ebony shook her head, blinking to clear her vision. "And please don't call be 'ma'am."

Daisy's eyes widened with fear, terrified that she might have offended her mistress' niece. "It makes me sound old," Ebony added with a playful smirk. Daisy giggled. "Leave those by the fireplace — I'll light it."

Ebony crouched down by the ornate marble fireplace and selected the best of the kindling.

"But you have no matches," Daisy said so quietly Ebony almost missed it.

Ebony laughed. "I don't need matches."

Daisy looked bewildered but left the room. Ebony peeled the bark off the twigs, creating a little pile of shavings, then rubbed the two sticks together until a spark came to life.

By the time Daisy returned, a fire was roaring in the grate. Agape, she put down her basket and stuttered, "B-but how?"

"Living in the woods teaches you a thing or two."

Daisy gave her an odd expression — what sort of Donahue *was* this?

"Back in a moment," she mumbled. When she returned, she and another maid heaved into the room a large tub, a third maid following after holding jugs of steaming water.

"*Another* hot bath?" Ebony blurted out. She so missed the bathing rooms in Faelynn.

"Of— of course." Daisy gave her fellow maids a look as if to say, 'I told you she was odd.'

They left swiftly as Daisy began to pull at Ebony's sweaty night clothes.

"What are you doing?" Ebony pulled away.

"Getting you ready for your bath."

"Oh. Right. Well I can undress myself."

As Ebony's clothes dropped to the floor, Daisy drew in a sharp breath, catching herself before it became a gasp. Her eyes lingered a moment too long on the gash across Ebony's shoulder blades, then darted away. She pressed her lips together, but said nothing, then stepped away obligingly and averted her eyes.

Ebony climbed in the tub in front of the fire and sighed, the warmth enveloping her entire body.

"You can leave me," Ebony said.

Daisy hovered uncertainly by the door. "Lady Donahue said to give you a bath—"

"And you have. I'm in it."

"But … when I give her a bath, I wash her too."

Ebony looked at the girl like she was mad, who flinched, taking a step back. A look Ebony had seen many times before when people first noticed her colour-changing eyes.

She had allowed Mary to bathe her a few days ago … but she had been so weak then, and there was something so trustworthy and motherly about Mary. Having a maid wash her was different. But this girl was only trying to do her job.

She attempted a kind, apologetic smile. "I don't need you to wash me, but … you can stay if that makes you more comfortable. I'll tell Lady Donahue that you did a *spiffing* job," Ebony said, mimicking the accent of a Southern Dweller. Daisy giggled.

"Daisy, is it?" Ebony asked. The girl nodded meekly as she

handed Ebony a bar of soap. "I expect you don't come across people like me very often."

"N-Never."

"I don't just mean my eyes. I mean — I'm not much of a lady. This," she gestured at the lavish room, "is all a bit new to me."

Daisy didn't respond, but Ebony could tell there was a burning question on her lips.

"I don't know why my eyes change colour. Always have done, since I was born."

"Do you— does your ... vision change as well? Change colour, I mean."

"No. I can hardly tell when they change. It's a bit annoying, actually. Means I'm a terrible liar. See, my eyes turn red when I sense danger — dead giveaway when I'm trying to hide something from someone dangerous."

"Does that happen often?"

"All the time."

"So ... do they change with—"

"My moods? I think so, yeah. Look, don't go touting it everywhere, okay? My aunt thinks the Jades might consider it 'magic', and you know how hot they are on that sort of stuff."

"They're on a witch hunt," Daisy replied, confirming Ebony's suspicions. "I'm so glad I work here where it's safe."

Ebony lowered her voice. "What do you mean, safe? What are the Jades actually *doing*?"

Daisy glanced nervously at the doorway before answering. "They're everywhere now, miss, not just the alleys and taverns. They've got men in fine coats sitting at the council table, judges in their pockets, collectors squeezing the shopkeepers. Even the rich folk are paying them off to keep their businesses untouched."

"So they run the city?" Ebony pressed.

Daisy nodded. "And they don't just threaten anymore, either. Folk who speak out go missing. Houses burned to the ground. Whole families wiped out to set an example."

"And their vendetta against so-called 'magic'? What's that about?"

Daisy bit her lip. "No one really knows, miss. Some say it's fear — they think anything strange or unnatural might threaten their power. Others reckon it's just an excuse to get rid of anyone who won't bend the knee. Even healers and herb women are keeping their heads down these days."

Ebony swallowed, her stomach twisting. "They always were monsters," she muttered, more to herself than to Daisy.

Daisy's gaze darted around the corridor again. "Keep your head down, miss. Folk say they've got eyes everywhere."

Ebony gave a stiff nod, but inside, her mind was burning. The Jades weren't just ruling the back alleys anymore — they'd become the city's iron hand. And if her eyes really did mark her as something "unnatural," she'd have to be more careful than ever.

Her stomach twisted with guilt. With the Shadow hunting her, how much longer would this house be safe? She closed her eyes, pretending to enjoy the warm bath but actually hiding her eyes, which, she presumed, were now a bright red. She allowed herself to sink into the water, her dark hair splaying around her. When she emerged, Daisy had gone, leaving her to bathe in peace.

She approached a wardrobe, hoping against hope there would be something to wear that wasn't frilly. She sighed with relief as she opened it to find men's clothing: a plain linen shirt, its cuffs a little frayed, a dark wool waistcoat with tarnished brass buttons, and sturdy brown trousers, their hems worn from use. It was a bit big for her, but a belt held it all in place.

She re-plaited her hair, fetched the parchment that displayed her family tree, which had been carelessly stuffed into her old sack, shoved it into a pocket and, with a grimace, rang the bell-pull beside her bed. Daisy appeared in seconds, looking Ebony up and down with a bemused expression.

"I hate to summon you like a dog," Ebony grimaced. "I promise I'll keep it to a minimum."

"It's okay. It's my job."

"It doesn't feel right to me. But I had no choice ... I don't know where the dining room is."

"Follow me, if you please."

Daisy turned on her heel, and Ebony followed her through a house that seemed to go on forever; walls lined with paintings, room after room, one with an easel and a half-finished painting. Down one flight of stairs, then another. Ebony peered into one room that seemed to be made of books, papers scattered across the wooden floorboards.

I wonder what Lord Donahue will think of me? I'm not exactly an upstanding citizen ... She could already imagine his icy glare.

"Not in there, that's out of bounds. The dining room is this way." Daisy led her to the third door on the corridor and opened it with a creak. "Here we are, ma'am— miss—"

"Call me Ebony."

Ebony smiled and stepped through a wooden door into a room with the longest table she'd ever seen, adorned with food of all kinds, a chandelier hanging precariously above it. Did they never worry that the chandelier might fall on them while they ate, setting the house ablaze?

"Hello, my dear," Mary said, looking up from a small book in her hands. "Come, sit. Eat. You look *much* better. I trust Daisy was good to you?" There was no one else at the table. Ebony sighed. She wouldn't have to impress Lord Donahue just yet.

"*Marvelous*," Ebony replied, smiling at Daisy impishly, who scurried out of the room.

Mary gave a quick glance at her choice of outfit but said nothing.

Before touching a morsel of unearned food, Ebony blurted out, "I have to apologise."

"For what, my dear?"

"You have to understand," she began. "I had to steal to survive—"

"There is no need to explain, my dear."

"No, I must. I can't accept your hospitality without admitting my, uh ..." What was the word?

"Past indiscretions?" Mary offered.

Whatever 'indiscretions' meant, it sounded right. "Yes, those. I had to do all sorts I'm not proud of. Though others like me would have killed you. I always did my best not to hurt people, unless I had to, to protect myself."

"And those you love? Your family? What would you do for them?" Mary asked.

"I didn't have anyone back then." This most mostly true. She'd had Hicks, but he'd always been safer than she was. He hadn't needed her protection.

"Well, you do now, my dear," Mary said. "And you won't need to steal ever again."

Somehow, Ebony doubted that. Things always wound up badly for her in the end. She smiled shyly and gazed at the food before her, most of which she didn't recognise. She spotted eggs, bacon, and toast. Those, she knew.

"Help yourself."

"So what do I have to do," Ebony asked between mouthfuls, "to earn my keep?"

Mary was doing her best to hide her look of disapproval. "My dear, you are a member of our family. You do not have to 'earn your keep.'"

"Sorry, but I do. I'm not comfortable being waited on hand and foot. Given all of this," she waved her hands at the food, "for nothing in return. Goes against my nature."

Mary studied her thoughtfully. "Well, I do have *some*thing you could help me with ..." Ebony waited, expectant. "I need some help in my study ... with a poem ..."

Ebony's heart dropped. Books? Reading? What had she let herself in for?

"Uh, I'll do what I can. Umm, where's Lord Donahue?" she asked, changing the subject.

"Away on business," Mary almost snapped. Ebony raised her eyebrows. "He's often away," she added more softly.

Silence lingered between them, both wanting but not daring to speak. Ebony broke it first.

"So, how much are we telling the staff about me? What do they know about my background?"

"Nothing," Mary replied firmly. "You are my niece, and that is all they need to know. They don't know if I had a brother or sister, and we must keep it that way. While I trust my staff with my life, your mother's 'magic' was once ... a hot topic, shall we say. Let's not bring it up again in today's climate."

"So … my mother's existence is just … covered up? Forgotten?"

"Well, my dear, so is yours. Your family line has left the archives and flown to who knows where. The family tree disappeared."

Ebony reached into her pocket and fished out a crumpled piece of paper. "You mean this thing?" she said, handing it over to her.

Mary's jaw dropped. "Where did you get that?"

"A friend, um, it was found, and—"

"It was stored securely in a vault."

"Not *that* securely," Ebony mumbled sheepishly.

"Well, well, at least it has found its way into the right hands." Mary tried flattening the wrinkled parchment and looked closely at the names. "There is *your* mother and our dear mother. Even our uncles are on this! I never met them, only my aunt, though she is living in Henley now."

Henley. Ebony had heard of that place somehow. "Your aunt is still alive?"

"I'm not that old!" Mary chuckled. "She is a fascinating woman. A Seer."

"A what?"

"Never mind that now. Look, your father's line is here, though I can't make out his father's first name. Can you?" Mary thrust the parchment into Ebony's hand, who stared at it, non-plussed. "You see it? There." She pointed at some symbols. Granted, they did seem a bit messier than the others. "What do you think it says?"

Ebony's eyes turned sea-green, and she looked away, holding the paper like it was a dirty rag.

Mary's cheeks reddened. "Oh, my dear … Oh, I'm so sorry. How embarrassing. Not for you! Oh, I really stuck my foot in it this time." She sighed. "Did the orphanages teach you nothing?"

Ebony shrugged. "We called it The Clink for good reason."

Mary sighed. How many urchins had been forced out of education and into a life of crime? And with the Black Jades in charge now, they were practically encouraging it.

"I tell you what. I'll tell you all the names on this parchment so you can memorise your family line."

"Are you sure you want to take me in like this?" Ebony blurted out. "I'm no use to anyone."

"Yes, of course I'm sure."

"But … trouble seems to follow me wherever I go."

"Well then, you won't be facing it alone anymore. Welcome home." Mary beamed.

But Ebony caught something in her eye. There was something she was hiding. Something she wasn't telling her. It didn't matter. Mary was treating her like family and keeping her safe. No amount of secrets could change that fact.

11

The days in the Donahue household were always busy. Mary had guests round for tea, a dinner party, important meetings in her study. She'd often disappear for days but would never say where she had been. Ebony didn't need to know. Her aunt was a lady of high society. She had luncheons to attend, people to schmooze.

The thought of it bored Ebony to no end. Small talk with a room full of Southerners? No thank you. For once, her colour-changing eyes were a blessing as they kept her out of sight. Mary couldn't risk rumours spreading, so Ebony stuck to herself or helped the staff in the kitchen. They soon got used to her milling about, and since she had nothing else to do (and Mary had specifically told them not to let Ebony leave the house), they gave her as many tasks as they could think of. Some she was adept at already, such as lighting fires. She was a quick learner but she got bored easily. She was a good enough cook, but not very au fait with the Southerner's food of choice.

Ebony enjoyed the bustle of the household and was only too happy to stay hidden inside. But in the quiet of the night, her dreams weren't so warm and inviting. She found herself wandering aimlessly through the Shadowlands, the Mother nowhere to be seen. Ash drifted around her, catching in her hair, and houses smouldered against the dark sky.

Every night she returned to the Shadowlands. It wasn't as terrifying as it used to be — a world of darkness she had grown used to, and a small part of her even enjoyed exploring the blackened streets. She had full autonomy now, choosing where to go.

Somewhere in the distance, eyes watched her — red as embers, patient and hungry. But she ignored them, turning away each time she could feel those eyes, like they were burning through her skull.

She knew it wasn't quite a dream and it was probably dangerous being there, but what could she do? There was no way to escape it.

Before her stood the tall tower she had once seen Henry run into, beckoning her to follow. She stepped closer and let the darkness envelop her. Red eyes stared at her in the darkness, big and bright.

"You're mine," a cold voice rasped in her ear.

She woke with a start, breath rasping in her throat, the taste of ash on her tongue. She was standing in the corridor outside her room, barefoot, the air sharp against her skin. She had no memory of leaving her bed, but there she was — hand pressed to the wall as if she'd needed it to stay upright. She crept back into her room, heart pounding, limbs aching. The fire in the hearth had burned down to embers and the heavy hush of the house pressed in around her.

The next night, the same thing happened. She found herself even further from her room, sitting on the floor near the staircase. How had she got there without noticing? Without waking up? She had never sleepwalked before.

She decided not to tell Mary. It would only worry her. And she definitely didn't need to know what had happened in the woods … the Shadow chasing her, the ring's strange blue light. She hardly understood it herself.

But each night she awoke in a different part of the house, no memory of how she had got there. One morning, as she came downstairs for breakfast, Daisy approached her carefully, as though afraid she might startle.

"Miss … Ebony?" Daisy began, eyes lowered. "You were in the kitchens last night. We found you standing by the hearth, staring at the coals. You wouldn't speak. We ... we guided you back to your bed."

And yet she had awoken by the staircase again.

"Oh! Yeah. Sorry, I didn't sleep well last night and I was hungry," she lied.

"You didn't respond ..."

Ebony's eyes turned grey. "I was just really tired and not quite sure where I was. New place and all, you know?"

But she had lived in this house for weeks now. It wasn't all that new anymore.

Before Daisy could respond, Ebony strode into the dining room as if she had no care in the world.

Mary wasn't at the table. It was to be another lonely breakfast, then. Where did her aunt disappear to? What could she possibly be so busy with?

The next day, as autumn light shone in through every window, Ebony wandered the corridors of the Donahue residence, gazing at the artwork lining the walls and relishing in the spongy carpet under her feet. The house felt dark, yet rich, with ornate wooden furniture, gold doorhandles, red floors, shimmering chandeliers, fresh flowers, leather chairs, tall clocks — every room seemed crammed with beautiful things. And Mary hardly took any notice of it.

But something told her she was being watched. Every corner she turned, the soft padding of feet followed closely behind. Did they think they were being subtle? For all Mary's 'you're to be treated as family', she clearly didn't trust her. Nobody ever said what they meant. There was always a hidden meaning or a lie somewhere.

She reached forward to turn the doorknob of a more plain-looking wooden door.

"No!" a voice called, and from out of nowhere, a maid came scurrying towards her. "You're not to go in there."

"Why not?"

"It's, uh, Lord Donahue's private study. No one goes in there."

Ebony narrowed her eyes disbelievingly but continued walking, pretending to gaze at the decor around her. She stopped short before a painting of a man with a large beard, and the maid almost tripped over her.

"Why are you following me?" Ebony said.

"What? I'm— I'm not following, I'm just ... I love this painting."

"Oh really? Who painted it?"

"I … I don't know, miss."

"Who is it depicting?"

"Well, I'm not …"

"You don't know much about this painting that you profess to love so much."

"Lady Donahue doesn't tell me these things."

"I'm sure she'd be willing to impart her knowledge. Why don't you go and ask her?"

The maid faltered, her eyes not able to reach Ebony's. "Well, I …"

"Go on," Ebony encouraged.

The maid scurried away, looking over her shoulder with a look of worry.

What was going on? Why was her aunt having the staff watch her but lie about it? Wasn't Ebony supposed to be the one keeping secrets?

"My dear?" Mary called from the other end of the corridor. Ebony was sure the maid had gone straight to her with concerns about Ebony's snooping.

Ebony approached warily. "Where have you been? I haven't seen you for days."

"Oh, here and there," she replied dismissively. "Join me in my study. I'd like to show you something." She beckoned Ebony to follow her. "Since you were so interested to know, that painting is of my husband's father. Come along."

She marched Ebony through the house and up a short flight of steps, then opened a door into a wood-panelled room adorned with lamps of all sizes, a large wooden desk, and papers strewn all over the floor.

"Take a seat, my dear." She gestured to two leather chairs by a roaring fireplace, both of which were occupied by a stack of books. Ebony carefully manoeuvred the old books onto the floor beside her and perched on the surprisingly uncomfortable chair.

Mary turned to her with a gleeful eye. She took a deep breath.

"I have been waiting for this moment for a long time — the chance to actually speak to the Demon in the Forest—"

"I'm not—"

"I know now. I've seen the real Demon."

That got Ebony's attention. Her head snapped up and she looked directly into Mary's eyes. Did she know the danger she was in right now? The risk she posed to her entire household by just having Ebony nearby? The Fae and the Sister had chucked her out when they'd worked it out.

"What do you know? What have you seen?" Ebony whispered, her eyes turning a dark shade of red, but Mary didn't flinch. It was like she hadn't even noticed.

"My dear, I grew up with your mother. Colour-changing eyes are not new to me."

Ebony gave her a grateful smile. She'd never felt so comfortable in someone's presence. This woman truly accepted her for who she was.

"When your mother died ... nobody could understand how it had happened. But I saw things I couldn't explain. The way your mother behaved sometimes — it was like she was possessed. Something lived *within* her. People were afraid of her."

Just like Sam. Her heart lurched, thinking her mother might have gone through a similar torture.

"But when she gave birth to you ... it was like the Demon inside her couldn't handle that light and love. Your mother was herself again, but she was very sick for a long time afterwards. Like the life force had been drained from her. And that was when it began. When my aunt ... no, I'll start at the beginning of *my* story."

126

Ebony sat back in her chair and waited, watching Mary twisting her hands in her lap.

"I had heard the rumours. We all had. 'They say there's a Demon in the woods.' Essentially, don't go in the woods, there's a demon in there that attacks carts. I thought it was folly until—"

"Until I attacked your cart."

"Exactly."

"I wouldn't have done it if I'd know you were family," Ebony said, though she wasn't entirely sure she was telling the truth.

"I know, dear. Anyway, the girl with the red eyes attacked our cart, as we had been warned, but as she walked away, leaving us unscathed — which we had not expected — I saw her eyes change colour. I had only seen that once before, in my sister. Your disappearance had always been a mystery to us."

"When my parents died, I was taken to The Clink — an orphanage."

"That explains it, then. Lost in the system, I suppose?"

"The orphanage burned down; any files on me would have been lost with it."

"Shame. Well, when we returned home, I was determined to find out more about you. I knew you were no demon, just a girl trying to survive. I tried looking for you to no avail. So one day, I threw caution to the wind and entered Rundlewood Forest. I walked until I saw people — a camp of sorts. I hovered behind a large barn, not wanting to be seen. And I heard a man speaking. I put two and two together and realised it was you he was speaking to."

She had been there?

"I heard him say who your uncle was — that ne'er-do-well Huntington Sparrow. Then it all clicked. You were my sister's daughter. I *had* to get you to safety. I was all ready to go marching into that barn ..." She paused, a familiar look of horror in her eyes.

"You saw it," Ebony stated.

"It was a massacre. A shadow — tendrils like claws ... those men butchered." She shook her head. "Every day, I try to erase what I saw from my mind."

"But the eyes ..."

"It's like they're burned into my memory. I'm afraid I turned tail and fled."

"I don't blame you."

"I wanted to find you, but my aunt ... well, I have spent almost a year debating whether I should search for you again, whether you were still alive. And when I finally struck up the courage to enter the forest again, gang warfare had spiralled out of control ... and you had disappeared off the face of the earth."

Technically, she's not wrong. Faelynn is on a different plain of existence.

"I was with the Fae," Ebony said, as if it explained everything.

"The what?"

"Never mind." She shook her head. One step too far for a Southern Dweller.

But Mary persisted. "The Fae are real?" she whispered.

"Well, yeah. Fascinating but terrifying little creatures."

Mary gave her a look of incredulity.

"You mentioned your aunt," Ebony said, changing the subject.

"Yes. I believe she is a key part in all of this. You see ..." She gave Ebony a stern look. "This information *cannot* leave this room, you understand?"

Ebony raised her eyebrows and shrugged with a nod. "Who would I tell? I have nothing and no one."

Mary nodded sadly, then continued. "My aunt is a seer. Through her poetry, she tells the future."

12

Ebony looked at her like she had gone mad. The ability to see the future didn't exist anymore. Even the Sister's powers of foresight were weak and unreliable.

"She has been writing poetry about the Shadow we have both seen. It reads like a sort of riddle, and I think we need to figure out its meaning. I think, with our combined experience, we could work it out. I can show the poem to you ..."

Mary sat on the floor opposite Ebony's chair, carefully spreading a pile of papers before her in date order. The bodice of her gown was fitted and plain, with a modest neckline, and the full skirt spread wide around her, heavy with the weight of many petticoats beneath. Once, she would have worried about it getting dirty — but everything had changed since she'd discovered the Shadow. The true Demon in the Forest. She licked the tips of her fingers and prised two pages apart.

"My aunt has been sending me these letters for over twelve months now, containing premonitions in the form of poetry, as is her wont. She feels ... compelled to write them, but hardly knows their meaning herself. Well, if she does know their meaning, she doesn't tell me. She asks for my opinion on what it all might mean ... but I can hardly make head nor tail of them! Each letter, she had another line for me ... sometimes a whole stanza." At Ebony's puzzled expression, she explained. "A stanza is like a paragraph, a section. I'll read them to you. Let me see what you think."

She looked up at Ebony, excitement dancing across her eyes. Oh, how she had longed for this moment. Ebony shrugged and nodded encouragingly. Mary began to read, her eyes roving each letter to find the premonition amongst her aunt's letter.

"They say there's a Demon in the woods, as dark as a shadow and black from head to toe. They say it was once a Dweller, but now is cursed by Darkness. It pounces when you least expect it and ..." She paused, finding the next section. Ebony's eyes had turned a bright yellow. "It pounces when you least expect it and can tear you to shreds with its claws and sharp teeth." She took a deep breath. "They say there's a Demon in the woods. It has no mercy and shows no fear. Its eyes are a fiery red. They say it was once a child, but the Shadowlands took it for their own."

"A child?"

"Hold on, there's more. That was only the first stanza." She scanned the next letter. "They say there's a Demon in the woods, a glare in the darkness, watching at night. They say it's as quick as the wind; a tearing, burning inferno. It feeds off souls to look for …"

"To look for what?"

"It took my aunt *months* to send this next instalment. Hang on …" She scanned a long letter. "Ah yes. It feeds off souls to look for its wick." Ebony felt the room grow colder. Wick? "Even the FaeFolk run." She had *seen* the FaeFolk run. "They say there's a Demon in the woods. From the shadows it came, searching the light. It has no heart, just a fiery pit. They say there's a cure that only Time can tell."

"You're mine, Wick," a cold, sharp voice pierced through Ebony's mind.

She jumped to her feet and glanced around her, eyes bright red.

"What is it?" Mary asked.

No shadows nearby, no red eyes, sunlight beaming in through large windows. "N-nothing," Ebony said shakily and sat back down.

Mary glanced up at Ebony with a wary expression. "This

133

is the next stanza. It isn't finished and … it's different." She took a long, shuddering breath, waiting for Ebony's attention to return. *"They say there's a Demon in the woods, lost to the darkness, cursed in the night. They say it has no thoughts, but thoughts are all it has. It seeks a heart, a body of its own. To live. To breathe. To rule.*

"I know there's a Demon in the woods. I've seen it face to face. I've felt the chills of fear and grief that follow in its wake. I know the way to vanquish, to make it meet its end: Three must stand where the light is drawn, their powers intertwined and strong.

But beware the dark tide that spills through the gate, where shadows rage and burn.

To open and seal the tearing night, the —"

The room fell silent.

"The what?" Ebony was on the edge of her seat, trying to make sense of the markings on the paper before her.

"That's where it stops. It isn't finished yet."

"It can't just stop there!"

"You see why I have been so anguished this past year? Desperate for answers and the next instalment?" She paused and gave Ebony that wary look again. "But … there's a note on the back of this letter. It says, "Shut the Shadow Door,

Wick. Don't let the Shadowlands reopen. They cannot return."

That was exactly what the Sister and Fae had told her. The pair sat thinking for a moment, then both began talking at the same time.

"Read it to me again," Ebony said.

"We should we go through it bit by bit."

Ebony nodded and Mary returned to the first letter. "Okay. So. *They say there's a Demon in the woods, as dark as a shadow and black from head to toe. They say it was once a Dweller, but now is cursed by Darkness.*"

"Well, we know there *is* a demon in the woods — and it is pure darkness. But once a Dweller?" Ebony racked her brains. What had the Sister told her about the Shadows? "Oh. I see."

"I don't. Ebony, what do you know?" Mary gripped onto Ebony's wrist. "Is it … a ghost?"

"Yes. Sort of. The Shadow is …" How did the Sister describe it again? "A lost soul. A ghost that has never found peace. It, uh, feeds on the peace of the living."

"So it was once a living person."

"But who?" Ebony wondered.

"We may never find out."

"What was the next line?"

"*It pounces when you least expect it and can tear you to shreds with its claws and sharp teeth.*"

"Yes, we've both seen that."

"Have you ever actually seen the Shadow up close?" Mary asked.

Ebony was so tempted to tell her the truth. Perhaps it was time? But Mary's eyes were wide and shining, her brow furrowed, her cheeks white. An expression of utter fear …

"Oh, no. Only from afar," she lied. An image flashed through her mind — the moment the Shadow had touched her. The Shadow's mark stung on her wrist and she covered it with her other hand. Mary didn't need to know about that — not yet.

Mary continued, "*They say there's a Demon in the woods. It has no mercy and shows no fear. Its eyes are a fiery red. They say it was once a child, but the Shadowlands took it for their own.*"

Ebony fell silent and brought her hand to her mouth, her eyes a murky yellow, like the blackness of sadness was marring their colour. "The Shadow was just a child?"

"A very angry child."

"A lost child."

"But what would make a child do such things?"

Ebony could imagine. She had seen unspeakable horrors and she was technically still classed as a child herself. "It isn't a child anymore. Not really. It has been twisted by the Shadowlands," Ebony explained.

"The what?"

"A land of lost souls. Shadows."

"There are more of them?" Mary whispered.

"Never mind that now." Ebony couldn't face telling her the truth just yet — that there were thousands of Shadows waiting to be unleashed, that what they had seen was only one of them, and it was very likely lurking nearby every night, awaiting any sign of Mary Donahue and her niece. "What was the next line?"

"The next stanza. *'They say there's a Demon in the woods, a glare in the darkness, watching at night.'*"

True enough, Ebony thought. Guilt stirred in her stomach. Should she tell her aunt about the danger she had let walk through her door? Ebony brought violence wherever she went.

"*They say it's as quick as the wind; a tearing, burning inferno.*"

They both nodded. They had seen that before. *"It feeds off souls to look for its wick; even the FaeFolk run."* Mary looked up at Ebony. "Is this ... referring to you? Its wick?"

Ebony's eyes turned red. "I don't know," she lied. Again. "But the next line is true."

"How can it be? The FaeFolk are a myth."

Ebony laughed. "They are anything *but* a myth. Does *no one* go into the woods?"

"Well ... they do to travel out of the Dwellings. But very few dare to venture in. And if they came out talking of fairies, people would think them mad."

"Well, I lived in the woods for years and I can tell you, they are very much real. As beautiful and sweet as they are terrifying. I think the Shadow is the only thing they fear."

Why didn't she tell Mary everything? Faelynn, the Shadow Door, the Sister. If Mary was struggling to believe in the FaeFolk, then an alternate realm might be a bit of a stretch for her. And if she told her she was hearing the Shadow's voice, she'd surely evict Ebony to keep herself safe. And this woman was nervous enough already about the outside world discovering her fugitive niece. She didn't need to be burdened with more worries.

Mary scribbled down some notes, then continued. "*They say there's a Demon in the woods. From the shadows it came, searching the light. It has no heart, just a fiery pit. They say there's a cure that only Time can tell.*"

"A cure to what? And how much time?"

Mary shrugged. "*They say there's a Demon in the woods, lost to the darkness, cursed in the night. They say it has no thoughts, but thoughts are all it has.*"

"It sounds ... sad," Ebony said. Was she really feeling sorry for the Shadow?

"*It seeks a heart, a body of its own. To live. To breathe. To rule.*"

No. All essence of sympathy fizzled out. It wanted everyone and every*thing* to join its festering pit of darkness and death. "The Shadow feeds off my friend's mind ... it's like he's possessed. It's trying to gain control of Sam's body ..." *But Sam might not survive long enough for it to manage,* Ebony added to herself. *Or perhaps that's why he's ...* She couldn't bring herself to even think the word 'dying'.

Mary's voice softened, a tremor betraying her fear. "Possession?" She shivered. "This creature ... needs to be stopped. It cannot exist in this world."

"Mary, it knows about our family. It is killing us off."

"I know. Every day I fear it will burn down our house next. And it seems my aunt does too. But I don't know why it is hunting us." She took a deep breath.

"I know why."

"You do?" Mary's eyes lit up with a mixture of glee, curiosity, and fear.

"The Three. It's hard to explain … But apparently I am one of the Three. I'm the Daughter of the Forest, and my mother was the Daughter before me." Mary looked utterly perplexed. "Basically, the Three can stop the Shadows. But no one knows how."

"Well, my aunt seems to know. Listen. *'I know there's a Demon in the woods. I've seen it face to face. I've felt the chills of fear and grief that follow in its wake. I know the way to vanquish, to make it meet its end: Three must stand where the light is drawn, their powers intertwined and strong.'*"

"'Where the light is drawn' — that must mean the entrance …"

"You know what that means?"

How much should Ebony share? *I might regret this, but …*

"There is a door to the Shadowlands. And … it needs mending. It has a crack. It has begun to open again."

"So the Three have to close it again? Is that the cure?"

Ebony shook her head. What did Mary's aunt have to do with any of this? "I don't think so … the Mother said that didn't work last time." She sighed.

"Your mother? My dear, you were too young to remember much of her."

"No," Ebony said, giving her a dark look. *Thanks for the reminder.* She scowled. "*The* Mother. The Three are The Daughter, the Mother, and the Sister."

"And you're the Daughter?"

"Yes." Mary looked at her sceptically. "I didn't believe it at first, either," Ebony added.

"I'm sorry, I still don't understand what the poem is saying."

"It's obvious, isn't it? The Three have to come together to close the door to the Shadowlands — or destroy them, or something." She paused. "But this poem … doesn't it seem odd for your aunt and the Fae to be talking about the same thing when they have no connection? Does your aunt even believe in the existence of the Fae?"

"I don't know. I never asked her." Mary looked deflated and stared at the papers strewn around her.

"What's the matter?" Ebony asked. She had been so excited just a moment ago.

"Well … I've been waiting so long to understand all of this … it felt so important. But now I have you here to help me … it makes even less sense. The Three? The Daughter? Shadowlands? I just don't understand."

It was time. Ebony needed help whether she wanted it or not. Mary knew so much anyway … and it would be helpful to have someone with her to decode it all and work out what she needed to do.

"I'll start from the beginning."

Ebony told her everything. Well, *almost* everything. How she had found the Fae Door (but not why she was fleeing), the story about the Three, the training she had started … she left no stone unturned. Except … it would be too much to tell her about her connection to the Shadow just yet — how it had touched her. She would explain that another time … hopefully before it was too late.

Mary diligently listened to her story and paused to clarify some things along the way. But she kept up well enough. And to Ebony's surprise, Mary believed everything she said. Not a hint of 'you're mad, time for the loony bin.'

"So that's where the colour-changing eyes came from?" she asked with a look of wonder. Ebony nodded. Mary paused for a moment to let it all sink in. "There's still a bit more of the poem ... '*But beware the dark tide that spills through the gate, where shadows rage and burn. To open and seal the tearing night, the —*'"

Ebony nodded. "That's what happened last time," she explained, ignoring the frustrating end to the poem. "The Shadows spilled out and destroyed everything. But the Mother said—"

"You know who the Mother is?"

"Umm, sort of. She's trapped in the Shadowlands. The Sister lives with the Fae, and they call me the Daughter of the Forest."

"So the third stanza is telling you — us — how to defeat the Shadows."

"Seems so, yes."

"So, if you need these two other people to do this ... why haven't you done it already?"

"The Mother is lost in the Shadow realm. Not so easy for us all to 'stand where the light is drawn'. It's hopeless until we can discover more and work out how to find the Mother."

"I'll write to my aunt. She might have the next line by now. Do the, uhh, FaeFolk know anything? Can you ask them? Do they … talk?" Mary had never said anything out loud that sounded quite so mad in her whole life.

"The Fae and I … we're not on the best terms at the moment. I was, uh, thrown out of Faelynn." It was clear by Ebony's expression that she didn't want to elaborate.

"I see." But Mary didn't see. She didn't understand at all. A lot of things about this girl didn't make any sense. "Well. I will write to my aunt for news." Mary gathered up the letters and huffed as she got herself to her feet and brushed down her dress. There was definitely something Ebony wasn't telling her — a *lot* she wasn't saying. But this was enough for today. The revelations about the FaeFolk and the Three were enough to keep her mind occupied for months.

13

A city of dust, ash, and darkness. A crumbling bridge and that shimmering archway, always calling her. It felt right to pass through it, like a rite of passage, a claw mark on her arm shining like red-hot coals. On the other side of the door: destruction. Figures of smoke and shadow looked up at her with their bright red eyes. Before her lay what was once a magnificent city, now forever decaying, like the aftermath of war.

A female voice rang in her ears. "You must remove the Shadow's mark." It was the Sister's voice. But how? Why hadn't she told her how to remove the mark? If she could remove the mark, maybe she could persuade the Fae to take her back?

But something told her that the Sister was wrong. The Shadow's mark was a good thing. This place no longer felt … heavy. It was dark, but lightweight, like she could move at will. And this time she had a choice. She could leave if she wanted to. It wasn't coaxing her in, but welcoming her. She would come back; she could come back at any time. Because part of her belonged there.

But in the far reaches of the city, Ebony heard a cry — a woman's voice. A screaming yell. Her heart began to race. Was that the Mother crying for help? How could she get to her? She

*was on a ledge on a cliff, high above the dead city. There was no
way she could get down.*

"What do I do?" she called to nothing and no one.

Silence replied, broken by another agonised yell.

An echo woke her. A sound running through the walls,
straight out of her dream. From somewhere in the house,
Ebony heard a strangled cry and sat upright, her eyes red.
She had been lying on the cold, stone floor of the kitchen.
How she had got there was anybody's guess. And the
screaming hadn't been in her dream. It was real.

Mary? Was that her screaming?

She leapt to her feet, the room in shadow, and ran to the
kitchen door, wrenching it open. The house was still; so
silent, Ebony wondered if all the servants had left. The long
corridor before her was dark; too dark. Should she risk it? It
could be a trap. The Shadow could be lurking in the darkness,
waiting for her.

Another scream rattled through the house. She *had* to
risk it. She retreated to grab a large kitchen knife and tiptoed
down the hallway, her heart thumping. When the screaming
stopped, the silence of the house rang in her ears. This

stillness was different to the quiet of the wood at night. No owls, no rustling, not even moonlight. Just oppressive, unnatural quiet.

It had been so long since she had been outside, confined to the safety of these walls. How she longed to feel the wind on her face again. Breathe fresh air.

She continued into an entrance hall lined with paintings, at the end of which was a large black front door — the front door she had come through, though she hardly remembered doing so. Further down the corridor, a light flickered from under a door. Lord Donahue's study — the room she wasn't allowed in. What was going on? Was this where the screaming was coming from?

She crept towards the door, dagger at the ready, and slowly turned the round, brass door handle. The door swung open to reveal a room made of books. The walls were lined with shelves, packed with books upon books, and a ladder stood in one corner. There was another door on the other side of the room that was slightly ajar. But there was no one inside the library. No one screaming. She would try another room.

Just as she turned back, she heard the creak of the far door and she leapt into the hallway and hid in the shadows. Her heart thumped as footsteps approached. She was testing her luck now. Whoever had broken in would surely see her. And she was sure someone *had* broken in. Why else would Mary be screaming? A figure walked down the corridor opposite Ebony and knocked on an open door.

"My lady, we're ready for you now," a man's voice announced.

"Thank you, Bastion," Mary replied.

Hang on. That was Mary's voice. So ... she hasn't been attacked? Who is ready for her? It was the middle of the night. Why wasn't she asleep?

Ebony heard the click of Mary's heels as she walked towards her. She flattened herself against the wall and held her breath as Mary strode through the study and opened the door on the far side. The moment Ebony was alone again, she followed them, carefully opening the library's second door to reveal a stone staircase leading down. She didn't like this. It didn't feel safe at all. But what was Mary up to? And what was the screaming about? She definitely hadn't imagined it ... though it seemed to have stopped now. She couldn't decide if that was good news or not.

She carefully made her way down the stairs and found herself in a large chamber ... it was *huge*; so huge, she could hardly see the other side. An underground hall. And she wasn't alone. The room was packed full of people standing before a stage against the far wall, all clad in black masks that covered their faces from the forehead to the lower lip. What were they all doing here? There were so many people, Ebony's entrance had gone unnoticed.

A woman appeared on the stage and the audience began to clap. Was that her aunt?

Ebony leaned against the cold stone wall, her eyes darting about. Something was clearly about to happen.

"My people!" her aunt called, and the hubbub of the crowd died down. "We unite today once more." Her voice boomed and carried far to the back of the hall, where Ebony stood. They had united like this before? Why had Mary not told her? "Hundreds have joined our cause. We stand as the biggest underground organisation the Dwellings has ever seen."

Mary paused and scanned the watching crowds, every eye on her.

"Our very lives are in danger if we do not stand up and fight against those who seek to control us and take all that we hold dear."

Who were all these people? Ebony tried to keep a look of confusion from her face, doing her best to look like she belonged there, though, of course, she didn't have a mask on. She mentally kicked herself for not having her own black mask. How had she got into the kitchen by accident? This night walking was getting more worrying … but she would think about that another time.

"We must gather our forces and act as one. We must destroy The Black Jades and all those associated. We must reinstate order. And we must fight."

The room erupted with cheers. The noise was incredible. Her aunt spoke so directly to the people, Ebony could not tear her eyes away. With all the energy she could muster, Mary cried her words so loud, it was like she was calling for the Gods to hear.

"The most precious possession you have is your own people! Do not let them go to waste, taken down and humiliated by petty criminals," she spat.

"For our people, we will never tire!

For our people, we will never lose courage!

For our people, we will never lose faith!

For our people, we will fight!"

The room exploded again with applause and roars of "Fight! Fight!" and "For our people!"

Ebony could feel the energy in the room and found herself wanting to join in. But these people knew nothing of what was really happening; the true threat to their world. A ruling street gang was one thing … but a swarm of shadows, hungry for souls, was something else entirely.

"Tonight we gather to share resources, to raise forces, to work together." Mary smiled and nodded and stepped off the stage, quickly disappearing amongst the crowd, who all began to mingle and shake hands like they were at a mass, anonymous business meeting.

So, my aunt is launching an uprising against the Jades.

She would confront her aunt tomorrow. She strode back through the study and into the hallway, frowning. Ebony had told her aunt so many of her secrets, all about her time with the Fae, yet her aunt didn't trust her with this. She had to admit, it stung a bit.

A cry ran down the corridor, and Ebony stopped in her tracks. She retraced Mary's tracks and found the room she had come from before giving her speech. Peering in, her eyes widened — with surprise and understanding. Three women stood around a bed that was stained red, and a fourth woman lay holding her newborn baby in her arms, tears streaming down her face.

So that's what the screaming was about. Another one of Mary's waifs and strays.

Ebony quickly retreated. She wasn't supposed to be up and about, sneaking about the house at this time of night. The maids must have seen her. Soon enough, the whole house would be on high alert to hide the illegitimate baby, to hide Ebony and her eyes, to keep everything under wraps. This house was a hotbed of secrets.

"What on *earth* do you think you're doing?" Mary whispered from behind her. Ebony grimaced but turned, her aunt's face a picture of worry. "If anyone saw you—"

"I'm sorry, I heard—"

"You're lucky it was me who found you here and not anyone else!"

"I know, I'm sorry, but … I heard screaming. I thought it was you."

Her aunt's expression softened a bit, but she narrowed her eyes. "What did you see?"

Ebony could tell her the truth. But Mary hadn't, so why should she? No. More secrets would only cause more problems.

She sighed. "All of it. Besides a newborn baby, I saw a large crowd of people in black masks, all to hear you speak and raise a rebellion against the Jades. Thanks for telling me, by the way."

Mary shook her head and looked away. "I tried to keep you out of it. Keep you safe."

"You didn't think that maybe I might want to help? That I *could* help?"

"We can't talk here, Ebony." Mary gestured her into the dining room and closed the door behind them.

"I know why you're rising up against them. I agree with the cause. I just don't understand why you hid it from me."

"But *do* you know? You've been gone a long time. You haven't seen the true state of things. You haven't experienced their ... their violence." Mary's face was stern, her eyes wide with fear. She continued in a whisper. "They have killed people for far less than harbouring a fugitive. They have whipped people in the streets for the mere *rumour* of magic. Your eyes ... if anyone outside this house sees you ..."

"Okay. I understand." Ebony looked into her eyes and touched her hand to show her sincerity. What had they unleashed? In their bid to destroy The Snatchers, they had allowed the city to become ruled by the worst criminals imaginable. "But I can help."

"Look, no offense, but you are an uneducated girl of little means. How could you possibly help?"

Ebony scowled at her. "I thought I was part of the family?"

"You are."

"Is that how you talk to all of your family, then?"

"Ebony—"

"An education and money isn't everything, you know. When it comes to gang warfare, it's all about who you know."

"Oh? And who do you know?"

"I was a Jade once. I know a lot of their members. I know their favourite hideouts."

"You— you were? You were a Black Jade?"

"Years ago, yeah."

"But … they're hunting you, aren't they? Why would they hunt one of their own?"

"I *used* to be a Black Jade. We fell out. But I can get a meeting with them easily, just by walking into the Common Market. Though nowadays … I doubt I'd walk out of that meeting alive."

"I … I didn't know."

"No, you didn't. You might've if you'd told me you're leading a rebellion. Seems a bit odd that I should tell you my secrets while you keep this from me. And your elusive husband? Does he know about this?"

"My lady?" a man's voice called from the hallway.

Mary huffed. "Ebony, I can't do this now. We will speak tomorrow." With that, she turned on her heel and left Ebony to the dark dining room.

When the house fell silent again, Ebony retreated to her room. But she didn't sleep a wink.

14

"For the last few months, I've been leading the charge against the Black Jades." Mary sighed.

She hadn't wanted Ebony involved — it was too dangerous for her — but she had no choice now. She sat on the end of Ebony's bed, staring at the patterns in the rug on the floor. It was early in the morning. She had spent all night tossing and turning, wondering how to explain it all to her niece, and couldn't delay it a moment longer or she might go mad.

"All those people you saw ... they wouldn't understand you. They're all from the South and West Dwellings. They ... they fight to gain control over people like you."

"People like me?" Ebony scowled.

"Commoners." She couldn't look Ebony in the eye.

"I see. They're the rich elite who aren't used to not getting what they want."

"It's not like that, Ebony," she replied, looking up. "The Black Jades rule the city now. They find any excuse to be violent. We don't want to rule over the Common Dwellings, we just want our freedom and safety back."

"And what does your husband think about this? Does he even know?"

"My husband set it up! He started it all."

"So where is he? Why wasn't he there last night?"

Mary froze and glanced at the bedroom door. She went to close it and said, "He works long hours."

"He isn't here, is he? I've not seen him once and I've been here weeks."

"I— he's— he travels -"

"You owe me the truth," Ebony snapped.

"He died. He's dead. He's gone. Okay? Is that what you wanted to hear?"

Ebony's jaw dropped, her eyes blinked, her mind whirred ... but she couldn't form words. He — what? She definitely hadn't expected *that*.

Mary folded her arms and looked at her floor, hiding her glassy eyes.

"The last few months have been ..." She gave a shaky breath. "A woman living alone ... it sends the wrong message. It wouldn't allow me to ..." She fidgeted with her hands as she looked out the window.

"What happened?" Ebony asked quietly.

"He was very sick," Mary replied with a faraway look in her eyes. "We tried to nurse him back to health, but …" She looked straight into Ebony's eyes, a tear on her cheek. "You have to understand, Ebony. A woman in my position without a husband …" She shook her head. "With all the danger on the streets." She sat down on the bed again. "I have done all I can to keep the rumours at bay. 'He's travelling,' 'he works a lot,' 'he's a busy man,' 'he sleeps in late,' … I'm running out of lies."

"What would happen if they knew?" Ebony asked.

"A period of mourning. I'd be the talk of the Southern Dwellings. Then I'd lose my rank in the rebellion. For now, I'm stepping in for my husband." She took a deep breath. "Then I'd be a widower with no prospects, no property or fortune of my own. I'd have to lose some of the staff … and they know too much. I'd be forgotten. Become nobody important, with no social standing."

"You really care about your social standing, don't you?"

"I used to. Now I just care about my safety — and that of my staff, and you. And social standing gives us more support, more safety. So you see why it is imperative that we remove the Jades. People will eventually find out that my husband is … And with the Jades in power, I am a sitting duck. But if I help overthrow them, *I* will be the one with the power. Not my dead husband."

Ebony nodded slowly. "And you kept me from this because ...?"

"Your eyes say 'we have magic in this household, come and get us.'"

"You don't trust your people to keep me a secret?"

"My staff I trust with my life. But the Southern Dwellers? Oh no. They will do anything to rise to the throne."

"Are you ... is Lord Donahue mayor or something?"

"No, Ebony, I meant it in a metaphorical sense," Mary said with a sigh of impatience. "What I mean is that most Southern Dwellers will happily knock me off my perch to take my place. And my perch is pretty high."

Ebony pretended she understood. It sounded a bit like gang hierarchy to her, but she didn't want to agitate her aunt any more so she said nothing.

"So there you have it. That's my secret, laid bare." Mary frowned, wondering if she had done the right thing in telling her niece the whole truth. "I am pretending my husband isn't dead so that I can lead the rebellion against the crime gang that is ransacking my city, the crime gang intent on wiping out anything they deem to be magic, while hiding my long-lost niece who has magic, colour-changing eyes and close ties with the Fae. Who are real." She gave a giggle of disbelief, and Ebony joined her laughter.

"I need a holiday," Mary announced.

"Let me give you all I know on the Black Jades. You can tell people you found this out yourself ... somehow."

Mary smiled at her, almost apologetically. "I'll get my quill."

A few minutes later, a nurse backed her way into the room, carrying a small wooden writing desk, and Mary followed, holding a large piece of parchment and a black feather quill. She sat on the end of the bed, the desk before her, and got herself situated.

"Tell me everything you know. If you can."

Ebony explained how she had been drafted into the Jades all those years ago, how they had taught her how the black market worked. She had learned quickly and had almost risen to the top, but the leader was caught and taken to the Clink. The new leader didn't trust Ebony. Most of them didn't. Who would trust the girl from nowhere with colour-changing eyes? There were no families in the Dwellings called Wick, she had no previous connections with any of the gang members or their families, and yet she had misled her way into to the innermost circle of the Black Jades. She had learned too quickly, they'd decided. Wasn't to be trusted. So they'd thrown her out. Some disagreed — those loyal to Ebony — but they had to back down to protect themselves. So Ebony had found a life for herself in the trees of Rundlewood Forest. Every so often, she had come across a Jade, and had some dealings with those she trusted, but that was that. Until she'd met Hunter Sparrow.

She told Mary how she'd been cornered by the Jades and pressed for information on the Bounty Hunters. She told her where their hideouts used to be, their favourite haunts, their hand signals and secret codes. They might have changed now, of course, but Mary agreed it was all helpful information.

It was late morning by the time they stopped talking, and Ebony's stomach grumbled.

"Come down for breakfast," Mary said as she folded away her parchment and rang the bell beside Ebony's bed.

When Ebony got downstairs, Mary sat at the dining room table, which was laden with food, frowning at a newspaper in her hands. She was still in her nightgown, her hair dishevelled.

She waved the papers at Ebony. "Help yourself, dear."

"What's that? What are you reading?" Ebony asked.

"A Southern newsletter. Doesn't reach the Jades."

"You look worried."

Mary looked up at her and again gestured for her to eat.

"The Jades are raiding houses again, claiming they have been ensnared by witchcraft. It's rubbish, of course. They just want an excuse to show their dominance and steal a few things. But we need to be careful," Mary said, eyeing her.

Ebony knew what she really meant. *She* would have to be careful that no one untrustworthy saw her eyes.

"I'm sure we'll be fine, dear." Mary smiled unconvincingly.

At that moment, a knock sounded on the front door, echoing through the house. Mary's eyes widened and she looked at Ebony as if to say, 'Who have you invited round this early in the morning?'

"I'm still in my nightgown!" Mary whispered fiercely.

From the dining room they could hear the maid answer the door.

"This house has been branded with magic. We need to search the property."

Ebony's eyes turned a bright red, her heart skipped a beat, and the world seemed to slow down — just at the moment when she needed it to speed up. The house stood still and silent. They had found her.

But how did The Jades know she was here? Mary's expression asked the same question. There must have been a mole at her event last night.

All Ebony could hear was her heartbeat.

"Quick," Mary whispered.

She pulled Ebony out of her chair and marched her to the kitchen as they heard the maid at the front door reply, "Of course, but please wait a moment. My lady isn't yet ready for visitors."

"We're not here for a social. Just let us in."

"Please be patient. She will be with you shortly."

Mary desperately tried to untangle her morning hair with her fingers as she said, "Stay here and keep quiet." She turned to Daisy who was standing in the kitchen doorway like a rabbit in the headlights. "She can't be seen."

With that, Mary marched out of the door to find something appropriate to wear. The house fell silent for a moment — a deadly, terrified silence, Daisy, Ebony, and the kitchen staff staring at each other, frozen and wide-eyed.

"Good morning," Ebony heard Mary say a few minutes later. "Excuse my attire. I wear my husband's old clothes when I'm painting, you see. How can I help you?"

"We wish to speak to your niece. We know she is staying with you."

Ebony gulped.

"Oh yes, she was, but she's with her family now in Henley," Mary explained.

"People say your husband is missing."

"Nonsense! He travels a lot for work. Now, is that all you came for or can I help with anything else?"

"Your house has been branded with magic—"

"I think what you mean to say," Mary interrupted, "is that you have unfounded rumours that something in my house is … 'magic'," she said with a false shiver. "But where is your evidence?"

"That's what we came to find."

"I see. And if I refuse to let you ransack my house?" A pause followed as the whole house gasped, and Mary yelped. Ebony could only imagine what was going on — likely a dagger to her aunt's throat — as she stood awkwardly in the kitchen, the cook frozen in horror and staring at the kitchen door.

"Well, if you must behave like that … But I can assure you, there is nothing out of the ordinary in this house."

The kitchen staff turned to stare at Ebony and her glowing red eyes. She smiled awkwardly and yearned to make an exit, but her aunt's neck was quite literally on the line, not to mention what they would do to the staff if they found out they were all lying and aiding the Donahues in hiding a fugitive; Ebony Wick, to boot.

The grandfather clocks chimed through the house as the Jades began their search. Where could she hide?

"The wine cellar," Daisy whispered. She held out her hand to Ebony. "I'll take you."

The kitchen smelled of coal smoke and yesterday's stew, but even that familiar warmth felt distant now. Heart hammering, Ebony let Daisy tug her forward and was once again whirled through the kitchen doorway. She could hear heavy footsteps overhead, floorboards creaking under the weight of boots, and the low rumble of voices too muffled to catch.

They paused at the end of the corridor, pressed back into the shadows. Ebony dared a glance around the corner. The hall beyond lay empty, lamplight flickering against dark panelling. But above them, another loud thud made her flinch — a door being thrown open, perhaps, or a chest knocked over.

My bow. My mask. The thought twisted her gut. If they found her belongings in her room, there would be no denying Mary's lie. Ebony dreaded to think what the Jades would do.

Daisy's hand was clammy in hers, but the maid's face was set with stubborn determination. "This way," she mouthed, and led Ebony further on.

They slipped through a narrow doorway and down a steep, stone stairwell. The air grew cooler with each step, heavy with the scent of damp earth and old wine. Ebony stumbled once, catching herself against the wall, her breath coming quick and shallow.

Above them, the search continued: voices raised now, something sharp and impatient in their tone. Ebony swallowed, trying to steady her pulse. The shadows down here seemed alive, each flicker of lamplight painting shifting shapes on the cellar walls.

At the bottom of the steps, Daisy eased open the door to a cold, dank wine cellar, the hinges groaning softly. She winced at the sound, but pushed on, drawing Ebony into the darkness beyond, cobwebs claiming most of the space.

For a moment, they stood there in the quiet, listening to the muffled chaos above: footsteps, a shout, the clatter of something falling. Ebony pressed a hand to her chest, willing her racing heart to quieten.

Don't let them find me. Don't let them find me.

"Behind the shelf," Daisy whispered.

Ebony had never seen so much wine in her life! Rows, stacks, shelves — all dusty.

"Miss, there's a gap in the wall behind this shelf … it's not very nice back there, mind, but it will keep you hidden. We just have to pull the shelf out first."

"Without breaking any bottles?"

They began to heave at the shelf laden with bottles, wincing as they clanked loudly.

"I'd like to speak to your staff," a voice said — unnervingly close by. It sounded like they were right above their heads.

Ebony and Daisy froze and stared at each other, eyes wide.

"Of course. I shall have them convene in the dining room."

They heard the boots clunk away down the hall.

"Go," Ebony whispered. "I don't want to get you in trouble."

"Lady Donahue won't mind."

"If you don't appear, the Jades might suspect something."

Poor Daisy's eyes couldn't widen any further. "But—" She gestured to the heavy shelf.

"I can do this myself. Now go!"

Ebony began to heave the wine rack, a horrendous screeching on the floor and the bottles rattling like they were trying to escape.

Daisy tiptoed up the stone stairs and went to open the latch.

"What the…?" said a gruff voice from above.

She glared down at Ebony and mouthed, 'Hide.'

Ebony squeezed herself behind the wine rack, barely able to breathe, and found herself beside the pipes in the walls. If she crouched down, she could hide *in* the walls.

Daisy opened the trapdoor again.

"Oh, gosh, sorry, you made me jump," she said, feigning surprise.

"What were you doing down there? You're not in the dining hall with the others."

"Lord Donahue asked me to find a specific bottle of wine for his dinner this evening ... I wasn't aware I should be in the dining hall," she lied through her teeth.

Ebony reached forward, fingers closing around the neck of one of the dusty bottles. The glass felt cold and slick against her palm, the faint smell of cork and old wine clinging to it. She hugged it to her chest, gripping it so hard her knuckles whitened. It was the only weapon she had.

"Let me see."

"See what?" Daisy's voice wavered, just slightly.

"The wine you were supposed to find."

Heavy boots thudded against the stone steps as the Jade pushed past her. His gaze swept the cellar with an icy sharpness, lingering on every shadow. Ebony pressed herself further behind the wine rack, her cheek brushing the rough wood, breath caught tight in her throat.

"Why is one of the shelves out of place?" he barked.

"Oh! Well …" Ebony could almost hear Daisy's mind scramble for an answer. "You see, I accidentally knocked a bottle off the shelf and it rolled to the back somewhere, so I was trying to find it."

"And you moved that whole shelf by yourself?" His voice dripped disbelief as he eyed the slight, wiry maid, candlelight glinting off his narrowed eyes.

"Yes," Daisy answered, with a bravado that sounded almost convincing.

"Well then, find that bottle."

"Uh, okay …"

Daisy stepped closer to the rack, the faint rustle of her skirts loud in the cramped silence. Her hand groped behind the shelf, fingers brushing Ebony's wrist for an instant — a fleeting, silent warning to stay still.

"It must be here somewhere …" she muttered.

Ebony slipped the bottle she was clutching into Daisy's hand, the glass passing between them without a word. Daisy's fingers closed around it, and she drew it out slowly, holding it up to the flickering light.

"Here it is," she said, the relief in her voice so carefully buried it almost sounded bored. Ebony congratulated herself for her accidental forethought. "I need to deliver this to the kitchen. So if you wouldn't mind ..."

As the trapdoor closed behind them, Ebony released a slow, trembling breath. The echo of the thud seemed to settle into her bones. But she daren't move. If they came back — if even a single board creaked — they'd find her.

So she stayed there, crouched behind the wine rack, the stale air of the cellar thick in her lungs. Minutes stretched out into something shapeless, until her legs prickled with pins and needles and her back ached from holding still.

What have I done?

The Jades were tearing her aunt's house apart upstairs, and it was Ebony who had brought them here.

If they find me ... she dreaded to imagine. *But if they don't, they might still take it out on her.*

A wave of guilt rolled through her chest, squeezing tight. Mary didn't deserve this. Nor did Daisy, now risking everything to hide her.

The darkness pressed closer, heavy and watchful. She drew in a shaky breath, trying to ignore the fact that she was in the dark, alone — the perfect place for the Shadow to find her, as it had done before.

In Faelynn, it had been kept at bay. But here, away from that quiet magic, Ebony could feel it coiling around the edges of her thoughts. Waiting.

She stared into the blackness, her eyes straining for shapes. The Shadow had no true form, but somehow she still felt its gaze on her skin, as though it was crouched just beyond sight, patient and hungry.

What if the Jades find me?

She imagined the sound of the trapdoor swinging open. Rough hands dragging her out, forcing her to her knees.

Then, unbidden, Sam's face surfaced in her mind. *Sam ...*

She had left him behind. Left him to face the Shadow alone, after all he'd done for her. Guilt burned sharp and sudden in her chest. *What if it's already taken him? What if there's nothing left of him at all?*

Her breath caught, the musty air rasping in her throat. In the silence, her thoughts seemed to echo louder than any footstep: *You've failed him. You've failed them all.*

She clenched her hands into fists, nails digging into her palm. But she stayed where she was: cold, aching, and alone with nothing but her guilt, her fear, and the faint, whispering edge of something darker, curling softly in the corners of her mind.

At long last, the trapdoor opened once more. Ebony held her breath and stayed as still as possible.

"Ebony?" her aunt called down. "It's safe now."

She sighed with relief. "I'm, uh … sort of … stuck." Her legs were so numb, she didn't know if they would remember how to stand.

"Hang on …"

Mary approached and squeezed her hand through the gap behind the shelves. Ebony grabbed onto her and unfolded herself, thunking her head on the pipe above her in the process.

She climbed out of her hiding place and embraced her surprised aunt.

"I'm sorry you had to go through that because of me."

"Nonsense, girl. You're family! And Lord knows we've got few enough family left as it is. Besides, you know full well it isn't just you we're trying to hide."

"But how did they know I was here?"

"We must have a mole in the house. But I can't deal with

that now." She began brushing down Ebony, her clothes grey with cobwebs. "We need to get away for a bit. Lie low. Be less conspicuous," Mary suggested.

"Away? Where?"

"We'll go to my aunt's. She lives in Henley."

15

They set out so early in the morning, it was still dark. Ebony rubbed her eyes and yawned as she padded towards her aunt's horse-drawn carriage, the horses snuffing and huffing as she approached. She couldn't count the number of times she had robbed one of these carriages — but the number of times she had actually ridden in one? Never.

She hoisted herself up into the carriage and nestled back into the comfortable seat, adorned with little red pillows. The inside of the carriage was made of a dark wood, two windows either side of the door, one out the back, with a small space for their feet.

The driver helped Mary up into her seat — a more graceful and careful ascent than Ebony's entrance — and two large, brown suitcases were strapped behind the driver's perch, the worn leather corners scuffed from travel.

Minutes later, the carriage rattled into motion, wheels crunching over the gravel track that led onto the road away from the townhouse. They were bound for the small village of Henley, nestled somewhere in the quiet folds of the Peregrine Plains.

As they set off, Ebony couldn't help the fear creeping in. The road curved towards the edge of the woods — the very stretch she used to know so well from nights spent lurking in the underbrush, waiting for carts just like the one they rode in now.

She didn't tell Mary what it meant to pass so close to the old paths, or why her heart quickened when shadows gathered between the trunks. The truth — that something ancient and hungry was following her — lodged like a stone in her throat.

Instead, she wrapped her cloak tighter around her shoulders and stared out at the blurred shapes beyond the window. Somewhere in those woods, the Shadow waited.

As they left the quieter lanes, Ebony glimpsed what the city had become. A boy no older than twelve ran down an alley, chased by two older youths.

On a street corner, a burly man with a jagged scar across his jaw barked orders to a cluster of younger lads, passing something small and glinting between them — knives, she realised with a sick twist in her gut.

They passed a row of burnt-out houses, blackened beams jutting like ribs into the sky, the stench of char still lingering even after weeks or months. It was eerily similar to her dreams.

Across the street, a woman swept her doorstep, her gaze darting nervously toward a group of Jade enforcers lounging by a tavern door. One idly carved a symbol into the wood with his dagger, while another watched passersby with a look that promised violence at the slightest offence.

They had no uniform as such, but you could tell them by the way they moved — loose-limbed and arrogant, as if they owned the cobbles underfoot and everyone who walked them. And in a way, Ebony thought grimly, they did.

As soon as they entered the woods, Ebony had to hold on for dear life to remain in her seat. The cart lurched from side to side, tripping over every stone, root, and fallen branch in its path. But her aunt sat still as anything. Ebony kept pushing herself back into her seat and held onto anything she could grasp.

"How do you stay so still?" she snapped, exasperated by her aunt's perfect poise.

"Years of practice, my dear."

Only thirty minutes into their journey and Ebony was yearning to walk the rest of it. The cart lurched to a halt and she sighed with relief.

"Are we here? Is this it?"

Mary chuckled. "My dear, it takes two days to get to my aunt's house."

"Two days of *this*?" Ebony's heart sank. They would be the most uncomfortable days of her life! "So why have we stopped?" she asked. But Mary didn't need to answer her.

"Unstrap the cases or you die."

The voice had a cold finality Ebony recognised all too well. She'd used that same tone herself, more times than she could count, on carriage drivers just like this one. Her hand twitched toward her boot, where the familiar weight of her dagger pressed against her ankle.

Shifting in her seat, Ebony angled her body toward the door, muscles coiled as though ready to leap down into the road. Her gaze flicked once to Mary, then past her to the light of dawn outside, calculating.

"Ebony, no, just leave it," Mary urged, her voice sharp with worry, then craned her head out of the window to get a look. When she turned back, Ebony was gone.

She heard an agonised cry, then the sharp, metallic clash of steel. Heart thundering, Mary leaned out of the cart — and for an instant, she couldn't breathe.

In the cold grey light of dawn, a lone figure moved among

a gang of thieves, black cloak swirling like smoke. The blade in her hand caught what little light the morning offered and her eyes shone a vivid red.

For a heartbeat, Mary truly thought she was seeing the Demon of the Forest itself. No — it was no demon. It was Ebony, her niece. And for the first time, Mary felt a cold, guilty relief to know that ruthless fury was on her side this time.

Ebony clambered back into the cart, a bloody line across her face. "Go!" she shouted to the driver, and the horses lurched into action.

"My dear, are you okay?" Mary pulled a tissue out of her handbag and dabbed at her niece's cheek.

"Don't worry, most of it isn't my blood."

Mary shivered. "My aunt will have some sort of ointment that will help."

Ebony slumped back into her seat, her heard thumping. She hadn't had to fight like that for a while, and boy it felt good. Her eyes were a dazzling red as she chuckled with relief. Her aunt's bewildered expressions only made her laugh more.

"So much for lying low," Ebony said. "I expect the rumours of the Demon in the woods will be alive and well again."

"Only this time, she's on my side." Mary smiled at her, a mixture of familial trust and fearful awe.

The uncomfortable journey continued until the road ran out of forest, and Ebony stared open-mouthed at the endless rolling fields that lay beyond the trees. She had always known the trees would stop somewhere, but she had never stopped to imagine it.

They were on a perilously high and narrow path, flanked by two steep drops, thick with little white flowers. Before them stretched miles upon miles of hills and valleys, long grasses swaying in the breeze, all different shades of green and brown, like a giant patchwork quilt. Had she stepped into some fantasy realm? Was she even awake?

Nothing — nowhere on Earth — could be as beautiful as this.

"You've never left the Dwellings before, have you?" Mary asked. Ebony could only shake her head in a daze as she longed to race down the steep inclines either side of them and run up the next hill. If Henry had been there, he would have joined her. Would she ever find another person who would understand her so completely?

They halted abruptly outside a fragile-looking wooden building, balancing on the hill pass.

"This is where we stay tonight, Ebony."

Ebony turned so abruptly, her neck cracked. "Huh?" she said, rubbing her sore neck, her golden eyes shining in the morning sunlight.

Mary frowned at her unladylike manners. "We're getting out here."

Ebony diligently followed her, clambering out of the cart. A short man rushed out of the building and grasped Mary's hand, a beaming smile on his face.

"My dear lady," he said in an exaggerated tone, stressing every word. "How good it is to see you." He gave a low bow and proceeded to collect their belongings.

Ebony smirked, and Mary gave her a curt look. "He is a kind man," Mary said quietly. "We will be kind to him."

"Oh, I'm sure he's kind to *all* ladies with deep pockets."

Mary gave her a disapproving glare, huffed, and flounced into the building. Ebony followed her into a slightly ramshackle inn, with windows that didn't appear to have ever been cleaned. She found herself in a pub, made almost entirely out of wood, it seemed, Mary and the landlord heading up a narrow staircase in the far corner.

She followed, wondering what on Earth they were doing

there. It was hard to picture Mary spending any amount of time in an unwashed place like this.

"This is your room, my lady, as always. And your ... companion?"

"My niece will need her own room."

"Right, yes, of course."

Ebony appeared at the top of the stairs, and without a word, the landlord ushered for her to follow him. The floor creaked ominously as he opened a door into a room with a desk, a wardrobe, and a four-poster bed.

"Thank you," Ebony murmured, and she heard him walk back down the hallway.

It was a small room compared to her room at Mary's house, but Ebony had never stayed at an inn before. She ran her hand up the decorative wooden bed frame and fingered the golden curtains surrounding the bed, before looking out the window onto the rolling fields.

"My dear?" Mary said from the doorway. "I know it isn't much, but we will be staying here tonight. The hilltop pass isn't safe at night, too precarious. Besides, this is the only stop between the Dwellings and my aunt's house."

"It's — it's incredible," Ebony stammered, turning her golden eyes to Mary.

Mary took a sharp intake of breath and stepped back.

Ebony frowned. "You say you're used to seeing eyes change colour, yet you still fear them like everyone else."

"My dear, I don't fear them! I am in awe of the colours you produce. Just beautiful."

Ebony blushed and turned away. "Oh. So ... where are we?" she asked to change the subject.

"The Peregrine Plains."

Ebony had heard of this place but had never been told what it looked like.

"We've got a few hours until we eat, so make yourself comfortable."

"I'd like to go for a walk ..."

"Of course, just don't get lost."

Ebony nodded and hugged her aunt on her way out of the room.

Outside, the air was fresh. She breathed in deeply and stared up at the open skies. Oh, how she had missed this, cooped up in that house for so long. She belonged outside, not caged inside. Every movement felt easier here. Not like the endless perfection of Faelynn, but light, like she could move faster and breathe better here. Even her mind shifted; a mental weight she had been carrying lifted of her shoulders.

She crouched down at the edge of the narrow path and picked some of the little white flowers, watching butterflies and bees float merrily from one plant to another. This place spelled 'freedom'.

She carefully began a descent down the hill, away from the inn, people, expectations, society, but before long, her legs took her and she ran, almost tripping, with wild abandon into the valley and up the other side as far as her momentum could take her, the wind rushing through her hair, a grin plastered on her face. She soon found herself in a sea of swaying grasses, and she realised she had never felt such peace.

And somehow she knew — there was no danger here. The shadows couldn't reach this far. She lay down in the tall grass and gazed at the blue sky above her. Couldn't she stay here forever? Make an existence travelling the Peregrine Plains, survive off her wits like she had done for years?

But the shadows were coming for all she held dear. For her forest, her Fae, her uncle, however infuriating he was, for her closest friends, for her aunt. She couldn't abandon them now. But she would come back here one day. Perhaps when she had inevitably failed and the Dwellings was a burning pile of rubble.

For now, she would let all thoughts of the shadows slip away, listen to the wind, and imagine shapes in the clouds.

16

It was with sadness that she climbed into the carriage the next day after a dreamless sleep — no red eyes, no burning cities, no foreboding dread in her chest. She braced herself and winced every time the cart's wheels almost missed the track, a vision of them tumbling down the hillside running through her mind. But Mary seemed as calm as anything.

It was late afternoon when, at last, signs of civilisation came into view and the track widened, the hills surrounding them on all sides. The village of Henley was nestled in a deep valley, the largest village in the Plains. The streets were cobblestone, as were the houses, some adorned with ivy or purple wisteria. Each house had a luscious garden, and animals seemed to wander freely, chickens squawking as the cart trundled by.

They stopped outside a pretty little cottage, Ebony stretching her aching bones. She clambered out of the cart as their driver carried the luggage to the garden gate, where a tortoiseshell cat sat pruning itself. It sat upright, eyed them dubiously, and stalked off.

Ebony watched as their cart trundled away. "Where is he going?"

"A nearby inn. He'll stay there until we need him. Now then." She approached the gate, which squeaked as it opened, and said, "Are you ready to meet my aunt?"

Ebony nodded, wondering whether she should be nervous or not. Mary knocked on the door, but Ebony hung back, feeling like she was intruding on a stranger's land.

"And with her she brings a companion!" a voice called from inside. The front door burst open and a shock of white hair enveloped Mary Donahue, parchment swinging from the woman's hands. "I had just finished a poem and begun to fathom its meaning when you arrived. It makes so much sense now! Did he make a fool of himself again? 'His bow so low, his nose almost touched the blessed ground she walked upon,'" she recited.

Mary pulled away from her aunt's embrace, and the woman looked up, her hands cupping her niece's face.

And in that moment, Ebony's world seemed to fall away. The face she saw before her — it couldn't be. Her heart began to race. She wouldn't be invited in and she'd have to tell Mary the truth about the Shadow — its touch. She'd have to tell Mary how her aunt had pushed her out of Faelynn, abandoning her to the cold woods and the Shadow, causing the sickness that Mary had rescued her from.

The Sister stood before her, swathed in colourful material. Her expression dropped.

"So this is your companion," she stated.

Had the Sister known all along that she and Ebony were related? She must have, especially with her talent for clairvoyance. But why hadn't she told Ebony? Why had she kept her identity a secret?

"Yes!" Mary replied, completely oblivious. "Auntie Tess, meet Ebony Wick, the Demon in the Forest. Although, you and I both know that is a load of claptrap ..."

"It's okay," Ebony said to the Sister. "I'll stay at the nearby inn."

"Nonsense," Mary said with a smile that was starting to grow wary and confused. "You'll stay here with us. Right, Tess?"

The Sister frowned, her eyes trained on Ebony. "Did you do as I asked?" she said.

"Oh yes," Mary replied, though Ebony knew the Sister wasn't speaking to her niece. "I brought all of your letters. They're all safe with me."

Mary carried their bags inside, wondering why her aunt didn't respond, and Ebony cautiously followed down the garden path.

The Sister held out her hand, stopping Ebony from entering.

"Did you do as I asked?" she repeated.

Ebony glared at her — her most fearsome glare. She knew her eyes would be a bright red — the kind of red that made people cringe and bend to her will. But nothing happened. No one gasped, the Sister just looked faintly irritated. Was it only her eyes that had instilled fear in people? She'd always hoped it was her natural prowess — but maybe people really were that prejudiced. All they feared was the 'magic' in her eyes.

"I — I haven't been able to. I don't know how …" Ebony stumbled. She had been told to get rid of the Shadow's mark but given no indication as to how to go about it.

"Don't worry, I've got the letters," Mary repeated. She looked at them both, nonplussed.

"Also, I have been busy getting to know my aunt," Ebony said defiantly.

"Your aunt?"

"Yes, Mary is my aunt."

"Oh, did I not mention that?" Mary laughed nervously. "Yes, Ebony is my long-lost niece."

So the Sister *hadn't* known they were related. Her eyes widened, and she genuinely looked lost for words. "Come in. *Both* of you." Reluctantly, she let Ebony pass.

The house began in a small entrance lined with jackets, cloaks, and boots, and a rickety old door that looked like it belonged in a stable led into the warm kitchen.

"Come through to the lounge," the Sister instructed. "I have tea or hot cocoa. Which would you like?"

"Tea, please," Mary replied, eyeing up the pair of them.

The Sister turned to Ebony, who stumbled, "Oh, I don't mind."

"Tea it is, then. Sit in the lounge. I'll be with you shortly."

The lounge was more like an art museum, the walls lined with old paintings. A fire roared before two small armchairs, and Ebony perched on the cushions.

"What is going on?" Mary whispered to Ebony. "You're both acting so strangely."

Ebony opened her mouth to reply but at that moment, The Sister entered the room carrying a tray of cups and saucers, and a large teapot. She quietly poured the tea and milk and passed it to each of them before settling in her own rocking chair by the fire.

"Aunt Tessara, you must tell me what is going on," Mary snapped.

"We have met before," the Sister stated.

"Of course we have — you're my aunt," she said softly. Sometimes, when her aunt was in a trance, writing the future, she'd become confused with her past and present. But she wasn't writing anything right now. "Are you quite well?" Mary asked.

"You don't understand. Ebony and I have met before."

"I— what?"

17

Mary turned to Ebony for confirmation and saw her chocolate-brown eyes. "Why didn't you tell me, Ebony? Why didn't you tell me you'd already met?"

"I didn't know."

"You didn't know?" Mary repeated, bewildered and disbelieving. "Would somebody please explain what is going on?"

"It's hard to explain—" Tessara replied.

"We have time—"

"Patience is key—"

"I didn't know her name when we met," Ebony added. "She was just …" Could she say it? Did the Sister want her identity revealed?

"Just tell me what is going on!" Mary's expression was fiery. Ebony had never heard her shout like that.

"I'm getting to that—" Tessara began.

"Can I explain?" Ebony interjected, and the room fell silent. She nervously cleared her throat.

"Mary, I told you about Faelynn and the Three …" Ebony began. Mary nodded, her brows furrowed. "I told you there was a woman there …"

"Yes, the Sister—"

"Well … your aunt *is* the Sister. Only, I didn't know her true name."

Tessara frowned at Mary. "You know more than I thought you did," the Sister said.

"So much for being able to tell the future," Ebony retorted.

"I told you it is unreliable. I knew you were coming, did I not?"

"You said so yourself that you couldn't fathom the words you'd written until we arrived …"

"Sometimes my prophecies are hard to unpack."

"Prophecies!" Ebony gave a bark of laughter.

"Let me get things straight," Mary snapped. "You spent time together in Faelynn?"

"Yes," Ebony replied.

"And, Auntie Tess, you are the … the Sister?"

"Yes," Tessara replied with a sigh.

"But don't the Three need to find each other or something? To destroy the Shadowlands?"

"Yes."

"So why on Earth did you leave Faelynn, Ebony?"

"I didn't *leave*, I was thrown out!" Ebony pointed at Tessara.

"You threw Ebony out of Faelynn, leaving her in the woods as bait for the Shadow?" Mary's eyes were wide, and Ebony's heart warmed to hear her aunt defend her. "You had both found each other and only needed one more piece of the puzzle — the Mother — to destroy the shadows forever. Why would you jeopardise that?"

The Sister turned stormy eyes on Ebony, as if to say, 'You haven't told her the truth, have you?'

Ebony's eyes turned grey, and the Sister replied, "Stylistic differences." They all knew it was a lie, and the room fell silent as unspoken words flew between Ebony and Mary's aunt. No, Ebony hadn't said anything about the Shadow's touch and neither did she intend to. "Ebony was being foolhardy, taking too many risks."

"That *does* sound like something Ebony would do."

Mary seemed to calm slightly and they all took an awkward slurp of tea.

"So what does this mean?" Mary asked.

"Not everything has to mean something," Tessara replied.

"But it can't just be a coincidence that you happen to have met before …"

"Well, it is," Ebony said, placing her tea on a side table.

The room fell quiet again, Ebony and Tessara stubbornly staring in opposite directions. Mary looked between them with a look of exasperation. "There is something you're not telling me, but I can let that slide for now. I would like to work through my aunt's poem and garner any understanding she can provide. Now then, can we do that and remain civil?"

Ebony pouted and gave a quick nod, gazing out the window. The Sister rolled her eyes and said, "I'm not a child, Mary."

Mary huffed and fished her aunt's letters out of her luggage, spreading them across the living room floor.

"Right, let's start here. They say there's a Demon in the woods … are you paying attention?" she snapped.

Ebony slowly turned her head, her eyebrows raised, and the Sister sat stock still with her arms folded.

"We're listening," Tessara said quietly.

"*They say there's a Demon in the woods, as dark as a shadow and black from head to toe. They say it was once a Dweller, but now is cursed by Darkness*". She looked up at Ebony. "Didn't you have some thoughts on this?"

"The Shadow is like a lost soul. A ghost that has never found its peace, so it feeds on the peace of the living. Right, *Tess*?"

The Sister raised her eyebrows at her, irritation in her eyes, but nodded.

"Who was it? The Dweller?" Mary asked her aunt.

"The one shadow you have both seen could be anyone," Tessara explained, "It's simply the only one that has managed to slip free of the Shadow realm. It matters not who it once was, but how to trap it once and for all."

"So it's true … there are more shadows?" Mary asked.

"Thousands," Tessara replied bluntly.

Ebony glared at her. She had tried to protect her aunt from the truth — the poor woman was scared enough as it was.

But Mary just shuddered, took a deep breath, and continued. "*It pounces when you least expect it and … can tear you to shreds with its claws and sharp teeth. They say there's a Demon in the woods. It has no mercy and shows no fear. Its eyes are a fiery red. They say it was once a child, but the Shadowlands took it for their own.'"*

"So say my premonitions," the Sister said in way of explanation. "We have all seen the creature, and we agree with this description?" Mary and Ebony nodded. "The poor child has been twisted into this being of darkness. There is no human left."

"So, the first stanza describes the Demon … or Shadow. The second stanza is a bit more cryptic," Mary said. "*'They say there's a Demon in the woods, a glare in the darkness, watching at night. They say it's as quick as the wind; a tearing, burning inferno. It feeds off souls to look for its wick.'* Is this …" Mary eyed Ebony beside her.

"When those words came to me, I hadn't met Ebony yet, so they didn't make much sense. I thought it meant it was looking for a way to ignite something … but yes, it makes sense that this refers to Ebony. The Shadows wants to tear down the dynasty of the Three, so they're hunting us at all costs. And while I've been here or in the Fae realm, Ebony has been the only one of us within reach, so she has been its goal ever since it discovered her."

"So you've been hiding from it in Faelynn because '*Even the FaeFolk run*'?" Ebony snapped. "You're admitting to being a coward?"

"I have *not* been *hiding* in Faelynn. I have been working closely with the Fae to work out how to find the Mother."

"*'They say there's a Demon in the woods',*" Mary interrupted, "*'From the shadows it came, searching the light—'*"

"Yes, it must have escaped the Shadow Door somehow—" Tessara explained.

"*'It has no heart, just a fiery pit. They say there's a cure that only Time can tell'.* Now this bit I simply cannot fathom. Why couldn't your premonitions tell us what the cure is and how long it would take to find it?"

"My dear Mary, you are educated in many ways, and cultured, but you forget your ancient languages. My name, Tessara, means 'time' in Ancient Ferolian."

Mary gasped, and Ebony's jaw dropped.

"So … '*only Time can tell*' … that's you?" Ebony said. "You can give us the cure to … to what exactly? Can you cure a Shadow?"

"No. I can't. No one can. You can only trap them behind the door."

"But how do you do that?"

"Currently, I don't know."

"But the poem says quite clearly that you know how trap the Shadow," Ebony said.

"Ah, but the poem also says that *'only Time can tell'*. Perhaps, in time, I will discover how."

"But we don't *have* time! The Shadows are breaking through the door already." Ebony's eyes turned orange with frustration.

"*'They say there's a Demon in the woods, lost to the darkness, cursed in the night. They say it has no thoughts, but thoughts are all it has. It seeks a heart, a body of its own. To live. To breathe. To rule'.*" Mary shuddered.

"Well, that part isn't too cryptic," the Sister remarked dryly.

"What are the thoughts about?" Ebony asked.

"It feeds on souls," Tessara explained. "And what is a soul if not the sum of its memories and thoughts? A Shadow is nothing but the scraps — fragments of broken thoughts, twisted into something dark and empty."

Mary went to continue, but Tessara interrupted her. "I remember this part. *'I know there's a Demon in the woods. I've seen it face to face. I've felt the chills of fear and grief that follow in its wake. I know the way to vanquish, to make it meet its end:*

Three must stand where the light is drawn, their powers intertwined and strong'. We know that. The Three must come together."

"'*But beware the dark tide that spills through the gate, where shadows rage and burn',*" Mary added. "'*To open and seal the tearing night, the …*'"

"That's the most frustrating bit," Ebony sighed.

With a cry, the Sister seemed to seize up, Ebony's eyes flashing red with alarm. Tessara's back was perfectly straight, her right arm outstretched, and her eyes were white — pure white.

"Get me a quill, ink, and parchment," an otherworldly, shrill voice said, coming from Mary's aunt.

Mary clambered to her feet, frantically looking about her.

"What's going on?"

"Help me, Ebony!" Mary shouted. "She needs a surface to write on."

Ebony jumped up, bewildered, and spotted a desk nearby. "Tess, you could sit at that desk."

"She's blind right now, Ebony," Mary snapped, searching through draws for any spare parchment.

Ebony touched the Sister's stiff shoulder, whose head snapped in her direction, her eyes swirling pools of white. "T-Tess, I'll lead you to a desk ..." Ebony was starting to understand why people found her colour-changing eyes so unnerving.

She persuaded the Sister to find her feet and carefully guided her onto the seat by the desk. Upon closer inspection, Ebony could see words and sketches scribbled across the wooden surface in ink. Tessara's arm sank to the table top and her nails began to scratch at the wood, forming the letter 't'.

"Don't — don't do that! You'll hurt yourself."

"She's deaf, too," Mary said, and she lifted her aunt's arm, placing parchment underneath it and a feathered quill in her fingers.

The Sister began scratching away at the parchment with the quill, a frenzy taking over, writing the word 'the' over and over till it filled the page, then clumsily dipping the quill into a pot of ink.

"What do we do?" Ebony whispered.

"Leave her to it. She's in a trance and will come out of it when she's ready."

"How long will she stay like this?"

"Could be minutes, hours, days. It's different every time."

They watched her as the next word started to form, starting with an 'r'.

"I'm going to look around," Ebony said. She couldn't stand to watch another moment of the Sister's agonising trance. She backed out of the lounge and hurried outside, taking big breaths of fresh air.

Beyond the little stone wall surrounding the garden was a row of similar cobblestone cottages, each with ivy curling around the doorframes and pots of late-blooming flowers on the steps. Smoke drifted lazily from squat chimneys, carrying the comforting scent of peat and hearth fires.

She wandered down the narrow road and turned the corner into the village square. A broad patch of green lay at its heart, ringed by neat box hedges and crowned with a weathered statue, its inscription half lost to moss and time.

Around the square clustered little shops: a bakery with golden loaves stacked in the window, a tailor's with a faded sign swinging gently in the breeze, and a small apothecary whose dark wooden door stood open to let the lavender-scented air spill out.

More cottages nestled beyond, their slate roofs speckled

with lichen. A handful of villagers paused to greet each other with quiet nods, baskets hanging from their arms.

A group of children laughed happily, playing with a skipping rope under the watchful eye of an elderly woman seated on a bench, her knitting needles clacking softly.

What kind of utopia had she found herself in?

She was in Henley. Where Tusting Hicks had gone to live. An odd twang echoed through her chest as a man walked by the village shop, but it wasn't him. She turned back and returned to the house, to find Mary slumped on the sofa.

"She stopped, eventually," Mary said as Ebony entered the lounge. "She slumped in her chair and could hardly speak. That's how it often is after a trance. So I got her upstairs and into bed, which was exhausting."

"So … what did she write?"

"Hell if I know."

She gestured towards the desk, where Ebony found the parchment, thick with ink; layers upon layers of words, some completely nonsensical. But one word stood out, emblazoned, bold across the page. "It says 'ring'," Mary explained.

Ebony's eyes widened, and she looked at the blue ring that currently sat on her hand. The blue ring that had scared away the Shadow. The blue ring that had come from her mother.

"We will discuss it tomorrow when we have rested," Mary said, her eyes closing.

Ebony went outside again and began to notice the greenery around her. Tessara's was the most amazing garden she had ever seen. Not perfectly designed and curated like those in the Dwellings, but wilder, teeming with flowers and vegetables. It circled the old house, out the back of which was a chicken coop, hens wandering about and clucking at her. She smiled and sat down on a small patch of grass behind the house as a chicken tentatively wandered up to her. In the far corner of the garden was a swing hanging from a tree branch. A feeling of utter peace swept through her — the same feeling of peace she had felt the previous day. She smiled, her eyes golden.

18

A whole week passed before Tessara was well enough to get out of bed and explain what she had written. Apparently this was normal; this exhaustion was a common side effect of her abilities as a Seer. She had told Ebony that the abilities of the Three had dwindled over the years, but Ebony had never expected the Sister's abilities to come at such a cost. Her own ability was now completely useless, and all she had to deal with was some odd looks from passersby and some suspicion. So what if people thought she was a demon? At least it kept them away from her. At least she didn't have to deal with debilitating premonitions.

While Tessara was resting, Ebony and Mary settled into Tessara's home like it was their own, finding a room each and making the beds. Ebony began tending to the overgrown garden, enjoying the labour of weeding and watering, tidying and planting. She enjoyed spending time with the chickens; curious creatures, however stupid they could be at times. A part of her didn't want to go back to The Dwellings — but she knew they'd have to eventually. The Dwellings was her home, and Tessara was used to living alone. She surely didn't want a wild demon marked by the Shadow moving in with her.

Mary kept the house clean and tidy and went to buy food every so often, but didn't have much skill when it came to cooking, so it was up to Ebony to make meals for the three of them. She searched through the kitchen and found enough ingredients to make her signature stew and even played around with some old recipes she hadn't been able to make since living in The Clink.

Mary would often stay upstairs during the day, sitting quietly by her aunt's bedside, spooning broth or thin soup into her mouth with gentle patience.

Ebony kept her distance, listening to the clink of the spoon against the bowl and the soft murmur of their voices drifting down the stairs.

She didn't feel it was her place to help with the Sister's recovery. The bond between Mary and her aunt felt private, built over years Ebony hadn't shared. Besides, Mary seemed to have it covered: smoothing cool cloths across Tessara's brow, coaxing her to drink, and simply sitting with her through the long hours of frailty and fever dreams.

In the evenings, they pored over Tessara's strange scribblings, trying to make out individual words. Ebony showed Mary her blue ring, since 'ring' was the only clear word they could make out, but they didn't want to make any assumptions about its meaning in case they got it wrong.

It was a quiet existence; too quiet for Mary, who grew bored easily. She wrote letters a lot and fretted a lot, but didn't share her worries with Ebony, who assumed her restless worrying was to do with her aunt's underground movement against The Jades. Mary was a socialite, and there was very little socialising to do in a village of people she didn't know.

"Come with me to the shops," she said to Ebony, who was digging at a vegetable patch while Mary sat on the garden swing.

"I— I need to finish this today."

"No, you don't. We've got all of tomorrow! You've hardly been into Henley. Come with me."

Ebony looked at her with nervous brown eyes. *If I go into Henley, I could bump into …* She wasn't quite sure if she was ready to face Hicks yet. But if she didn't go with her aunt now, she wouldn't get a moment's peace all day.

She sighed. "Fine. But let me clean myself up first."

Mary beamed at her. "You've done a lovely job with the

garden, my dear. A shame we don't have much of a garden at home."

Home. Mary referred to it as if it was Ebony's home, too. Was it? Did she feel at home in her aunt's huge town house? Not particularly.

As they left the house, Mary hooked her arm through Ebony's. "I've found a darling little modiste and thought it was high time we got you some clothes of your own."

"I don't need any clothes."

"You do." Ebony huffed and Mary rolled her eyes. "You don't have to wear dresses, but you do need something that fits and isn't tattered."

She marched Ebony into a little shop, the exterior painted blue, and Ebony's chest gave an uncomfortable lurch as she saw a tall man with short brown hair at the till. She froze, her eyes turning grey, but as he turned, her beating heart slowed as she realised it wasn't him.

"What's wrong, my dear?" Mary asked.

"N-nothing."

They spent the best part of an hour sizing up Ebony and putting her into various outfits, most of which she detested. She emerged from the shop wearing a long, brown, leather riding coat with silver buttons, black breeches, knee-length leather boots, and a white cotton shirt under a brown waistcoat. She couldn't believe how much her aunt had spent on her!

"There. You may look like a man, but at least you are now presentable," her aunt smiled. "Let's see what the farmers' market has in store for us today."

They stepped back out into the pale light, the air cool and fresh after the cramped warmth of the shop. The narrow street led them straight to the village green, where Henley's weekly farmers' market had come alive.

Wooden stalls crowded the square in cheerful disorder, draped with striped awnings and worn canvas. Baskets overflowed with apples, dusty carrots still crowned with leaves, and bunches of herbs tied with twine. A butcher's cart offered pies and cured meats, while further down, a dairywoman stood behind neat rows of cheeses, the rinds powdered white with age.

The scent of fresh bread mingled with woodsmoke and the faint tang of livestock. Chickens clucked from wicker crates, and a drover guided two stubborn goats past a stall selling bolts of homespun cloth.

Mary moved easily among the crowd, nodding politely to

stallholders and pausing to examine jars of honey and folded linens. Ebony trailed beside her, still half lost in thought, one hand brushing the smooth leather of her new coat as though she couldn't quite believe it was hers.

Children darted between the stalls with sticky fingers, and somewhere a fiddler scraped out a tune light enough to catch on the afternoon breeze. For a fleeting moment, it almost felt like a life Ebony might have had; simple, bustling, ordinary.

Mary steered them from stall to stall with quiet certainty, pausing to smell bunches of rosemary and thyme, and pressing gently at the sides of pears to test for ripeness. They bought a round of crumbly white cheese wrapped in waxed paper, a crusty loaf that still felt warm from the oven, and a small jar of honey that glowed amber.

At the butcher's cart, Mary selected a cut of lamb for supper, her gloved hand steady as she pointed out the piece she wanted. Ebony, less helpful, carried the growing weight of cloth bags slung over her shoulder, though she did sneak a small apple tart into their purchases when Mary wasn't looking.

They lingered near a flower seller whose stall spilled over with daisies, lavender, and bunches of pale heather, their scent mingling sweetly with the sharper tang of cured meats drifting from the next stall.

By the time they turned back toward the Sister's house, the street was starting to quiet, shadows growing longer across the cobbles. Ebony's feet ached in her new boots, the press of people and the warmth of the coat making her sluggish.

She was exhausted when they finally reached the house, shoulders aching from the weight of the bags. Dropping them in the hallway, she slumped down onto one of the sofas, boots scuffing against the rug. In the kitchen, she could hear her aunt gently unpacking their spoils.

Ebony turned as she heard footsteps coming down the stairs.

"I'm ready now," a rough, crackly voice said.

"Oh, hi," Ebony said, sitting upright as the Sister entered the lounge. "How are you feeling?"

"I've been better, but I'm recovering. It's time we riddled out my latest premonition. Have you had a chance to look at it?"

"Umm, well, yes, but …" Ebony paused and glanced over at the desk where the Sister's wild scribblings sat.

"But what?"

"It— it doesn't really make any sense to us."

The Sister went to pick up the paper and frowned. "What do you mean? The words are written here quite clearly."

"All we could make out was 'ring.'"

At that moment, Mary wandered into the lounge and yelped as she almost collided with her aunt. "You're awake! And downstairs! Shouldn't you be in bed?"

"I'm feeling a lot more myself now. I think we ought to work through my poem together. Ebony tells me you've hardly read a word of it — you could have got started on riddling it out, you know."

"We tried," Mary explained, shooting Ebony a look of confusion. "But it doesn't really make any sense to us …"

"The words are written here clear as day …"

"How? To us it's just a page of wild scribblings."

"Ah. I see. Yes, I recall that happening once before. Right, well I'll write out what I can see and then read it to you."

Mary gave Ebony a quizzical look, who shrugged, and they watched Tessara decipher the mess of ink into a fully formed stanza of a poem.

"So, what does it say?" Mary asked. Ebony could see excitement building in her eyes.

"Well, my last poem ended with '*To open and seal the tearing night, the —*'"

"Yes ... so how does it end?"

"'*To open and seal the tearing night, the ring is the key to turn.*

"*To destroy the Demon in the woods, gather strength and forge the light. With the Wick, unite the realms: the city, forest, and Fae. Time draws near, the shadows rise, when day gives way to endless night.*

"*To destroy the Demon in the woods, seek the truth and harness the flame. The door to darkness trembles now, its bonds begin to strain.*'" The room fell silent. "This time ... it feels like it's the end. Like there's no more to come."

"How do you know?" Ebony asked.

"I can just ... feel that it is done. The message has been given."

"Read it again. Slower this time."

"'*To open and seal the tearing night, the ring is the key to turn.*'"

"The ring ..." Ebony said. "Do you think it is referring to this ring?" She held up her hand, and the Sister gasped. "The Daughter's ring! Where did you get that?"

213

Ebony's eyes turned grey with guilt. "Well, actually, I, err—"

"I inherited it from my sister when she died," Mary interjected, "and Ebony stole it from me when she attacked our cart in the woods. That was how we first met." Mary didn't seem upset about what had happened — it was so matter-of-fact with her.

The Sister raised her eyebrows and pursed her lips with disapproval. She turned to Ebony. "So you had it all along in Faelynn? Why didn't you tell me?"

"I— I didn't know it was the Daughter's ring. I mean, well, it was my mother's ring, and I'm *her* daughter and *the* Daughter, so I suppose I should have put two and two together …"

"You clever thing!" Tessara beamed. Was it the first time she had actually complimented Ebony? "I think that's *exactly* what the poem is referring to. May I see it?"

Ebony nodded, pulling it off her finger and handing it to The Sister.

"Has it ever …" Tessara began, not quite sure how to ask the question. "Have you seen it do anything? Anything a ring shouldn't normally do?"

"Something happened once ..." Ebony replied. "Quite recently, actually. The Shadow was chasing me through the woods — before I came to Mary's house. As it approached, I held up my hand with this ring on my finger and it screamed and fled."

Mary's eyes widened, her face paling a shade. "You never told me it had chased you! You could have ... it could have ..."

"The ring is the key to the Shadow Door," Tessara explained. "The Shadow fears it. That's how you'll get into the Shadowlands and protect yourself while you're there."

"But what about the rest of the poem? What does it all mean?" Mary asked.

"*'To destroy the Demon in the woods, gather strength and forge the light. With the Wick, unite the realms: the city, forest, and Fae. Time draws near, the shadows rise, when day gives way to endless night.'*"

"What does that mean? 'Forge the light'?" Mary asked.

"I assume it's to do with the Fae?" Ebony suggested.

"Yes, I think the light they create will help us somehow," Tessara agreed.

"They can create light?" Mary asked, but they both ignored her. They hardly knew how the Faelight worked, anyway.

"*'With the Wick'* — that's me again, isn't it?" Ebony frowned.

"Yes, I believe so."

"So I have to unite the realms — city, forest, and Fae?" Ebony echoed, the weight of the words sitting heavy on her shoulders.

"It appears so," Mary replied quietly, her gaze steady and serious.

"How in Atlaan's great name am I supposed to do that? Who might that even refer to? 'The city' — the gangs? The government? The urchins?" Ebony's voice cracked slightly as she spoke.

The city flickered in her mind like a restless beast — a sprawling maze of soot-darkened rooftops, shadowed alleyways, and the constant murmur of danger. Gangs ruled the streets with iron fists and the urchins survived by their wits and quick knives.

The forest pressed in on her thoughts. Did this mean she'd have to face The Foryx again? Reunite the fractured Bounty Hunters? The very idea felt impossible.

And the Fae — they weren't even speaking to her.

"'Only Time will tell'?" Mary suggested.

Tessara continued, "'*To destroy the Demon in the woods, seek the truth and harness the flame*'. Ebony, you are the flame. '*The door to darkness trembles now, its bonds begin to strain*.' Yes, the door is breaking open."

"So ... so what does this mean? What do we do?" Ebony asked.

"We? I think it's all down to you now," the Sister said, giving Ebony a look of expectation.

"What? But I don't know how to do any of that. They all hate me. The city wants me in the Clink — or dead, the Fae threw me out, and the Forest ... it isn't a safe place for me anymore. They all hate me. Everyone."

"And we're running out of time," Mary said gravely. "If the Shadow Door opens and nobody is there to protect the Fae ... as the poem says, '*the shadows rise, when day gives way to endless night*.'"

The Sister put a hand on Ebony's shoulder. "One day, you'll find that the cost of staying safe is far greater than the risk of stepping forward."

Ebony sank back onto the worn couch, her chest heaving. Her hands trembled in her lap, fingers clenched tight like she was trying to hold herself together.

"Oh, my dear." Mary eased down beside her, her voice soft and steady as she wrapped her arms around Ebony's shoulders, pulling her close. "I'll be here with you all the way. I'll help you do it all."

But Ebony shook her head. "It's just ... why me? Why does all of this have to fall on me? It's too much." Tears spilled over, tracing warm trails down her cheeks. "You don't know what my life has been like. All I've ever known is survival, how to keep myself alive and safe. And now you're telling me to do the opposite?"

Mary opened her mouth to speak, but Ebony pressed on, and it all came tumbling out in a rush of broken sentences and sobs.

"After growing up in the Clink — the worst of all prisons in The Dwellings — I lost my best friend in a fire, which is where I lost all records of my existence, m-my family, even my birthday!" Her voice caught. "I was taken in by The Jades, who then betrayed me, and I had to run into Rundlewood Forest and survive off my own wits for *years*. I was called a Demon, forced to kill and steal to survive.

"All I had was my friend Tusting, and then even he abandoned me, and the Bounty Hunters were all brutally killed by the Fae — yes, they're more dangerous than you think — and I ran away to live with my number one enemy who had tortured me, all with the promise that I'd find more of my family.

"Turned out he was …" Her hands trembled as she fought for composure, "a really great person, he was just possessed by the Shadow that has been systematically killing off my family for decades. And then when … when I was trapped in a barn with the Shadow, it …" she faltered. Should she tell Mary the truth about the Shadow's mark?

"I ran away again and found the Fae, and I thought I was safe in Faelynn, but the Fae threw me out and left me to fend for myself again, and the Shadow chased me through the woods until I found the wooden village, but then I learned that Sam is *dying* because of the Shadow … and I know it's my fault, but still I ran and found my aunt — an actual living relative — who w-welcomed me in like long-lost family—"

"You *are* long-lost family, my dear -" Mary whispered, pressing a kiss to Ebony's hair.

Ebony sobbed anew, the sound raw and trembling. "And then The Jades raided your house because of me and we came here to understand this cryptic poem you've written, only to discover that *I* have to save the whole world from death by shadow." She heaved a few deep, shuddering breaths, ignoring the stunned looks exchanged between Mary and Tessara. "It's just … all too much. Too much."

Tessara, sitting quietly nearby, reached out a frail hand and lightly touched Ebony's arm. Her pale eyes held a rare softness. "You didn't say any of this in Faelynn."

"Of course I didn't. I was safe for the first time in my life and I didn't want to risk losing that. I'm so tired of fighting for my survival ... but in all honesty, I'm nothing without it. There's no purpose to me other than staying alive. And now you say I've got to save the world from destruction?" She gave a look of exasperation, her eyes a darker red than ever before.

"My dear, you are more than just survival." Mary squeezed her shoulders. "You're my niece, my dear sister's daughter. You're *the* Daughter, friend of the Fae, the Dwellings' first highwaywoman. You're scared, and that's understandable. But maybe this premonition *is* your purpose? And once it's over, you'll be free and at peace. Ready to properly begin living your life."

"You matter to all of us more than you could ever understand," the Sister added.

Ebony curled up on the sofa, cradling her aching head.

"Let her sleep," Mary suggested, and the two women stepped out of the room to admire Ebony's work in the garden.

19

It was with a heavy heart that Ebony left Henley the next day, but it was time they went back to The Dwellings. The morning air was cool and still, dew beading on the grass and the low stone garden wall. As they heaved their luggage to the waiting cart — now burdened with even more bags of shopping Mary had collected throughout the week — the Sister beckoned Ebony aside.

They stepped onto the path that wound through the small front garden, where pale heather and late-blooming lavender spilled over the edges of the beds.

"There is still the small matter of the Shadow's mark on your arm," the Sister murmured, her voice low but firm. "With it, the Shadow will take your mind before you even find the Mother."

Ebony's chest tightened, breath catching painfully. The words struck like cold iron. With the mark on her arm, the Shadow already had a claim on her mind — the sleepwalking, the voices, the creeping dark thoughts ... *She was on the same path as Sam.* Realisation crashed over her: the same Shadow that had slowly consumed him was already winding its way into her mind, silent and patient.

"You have a connection with the Mother in your dreams, don't you?"

"Sometimes, yes."

"You must find her and get her ready. She must know we are building a force."

"I'm not going back to that place willingly." Ebony shivered slightly, her gaze dropping to the moss-dappled stones at her feet.

"You can no longer avoid it," the Sister said gently, though her words carried the weight of inevitability. "The Fae and I have realised: searching in dreams is no longer enough. You will have to cross into the Shadowlands yourself — to find and free the Mother and unite the Three."

Ebony's breath caught painfully, and she shook her head, her dark hair falling into her eyes. "Into the Shadowlands? *Truly* go there?" A nauseating feeling of dread settled in her stomach. "Why can't you go?"

"The poem states that the Daughter's ring is the key. It will only work when worn by the Daughter."

"So I have to go in alone?"

"I'm afraid so. But you can't do any of that with the

222

Shadow's mark. Their darkness will claim you and you'll never be able to leave. You must remove it."

"But how?" Ebony whispered, glancing uneasily toward Mary, who stood by the cart giving instructions to the driver.

"You will find a way." The Sister's gaze was unwavering, though lines of worry framed her pale eyes.

"And when will the Three unite?" Ebony pressed, her voice tight with frustration.

"You will know when it is time."

"That's not very helpful, you know." Ebony's attempt at defiance came out thin, almost weary.

The Sister frowned at her, her expression softening into something between reproach and concern.

Around them, the garden lay hushed, the quiet broken only by the distant clop of hooves on cobbles. How was she supposed to build a force when she was being hunted everywhere she went? Even if she did manage to gather a force of city, forest, and Fae, even if they did all come together, their plan wouldn't work with the stupid Shadow's mark on her arm.

"You will find a way," the Sister said, as if reading Ebony's mind. "And I will come to your call when the time comes."

"Cryptic as always."

"Sometimes words come to me unbidden, and I must speak them — even when their meaning is hidden," she replied, a look of curiosity and contemplation in her eyes.

"So when *will* the time come?" Ebony asked.

"Only time will tell."

"But you *are* Time ... can't you tell yourself whenever you like?"

"It doesn't work like that I'm afraid. Now go. Your aunt is getting fidgety."

Ebony walked to the end of the garden path, but paused and turned back.

"I'll miss this place, you know. And your garden."

"It will miss you too."

Ebony nodded and gave a smile before joining her aunt on the cart, and they waved goodbye as the uncomfortable journey home began. They returned the way they had come — along the perilously thin mountain pass, one night in the hotel surrounded by valleys, and back through the forest, until eventually Mary's town house hove into view. It was dark when they arrived, and Ebony stretched uncomfortably, looking forward to a soft bed.

In the dead of night, she slept soundly in the bed that had rescued her — the darkness no longer haunting but comforting and safe. She had come to think of Mary's house as 'home' the moment they'd returned from Henley. Warm, kind, loving, protected — she imagined this was what her childhood should have felt like.

A tap-tapping dragged her from her slumber, and she groaned. Was it morning already? She lay with her eyes closed, listening to the irregular tapping on her window.

Then she heard her name.

"Ebony."

Come to me. You're mine, a voice whispered in her head.

And just like that, all her fears came surging back. Red eyes in the night.

She leapt out of bed and stared around the dark room. But there were no red eyes, no creeping shadows. It must have been a bad dream, she surmised. At least she had woken in her bed and not on the kitchen floor.

But there it was again. A tapping on her window.

In her night gown, she tentatively tiptoed over and peered through her curtains. Below the window stood a figure — tall and strong, but bedraggled. He was throwing pebbles at her window, the faint light of a nearby gas lamp shone across his features — a ginger beard and long ginger hair, pulled back by a hair tie.

It couldn't be.

She slowly and quietly opened her window and leaned out. Her voice a harsh whisper, she hissed, "What the hell are you doing here?"

He beamed at her. Hunter Sparrow. Her wayward, untrustworthy, long-lost uncle. She scowled as he beckoned for her to join him in the street.

However much she didn't want to speak to him, she had to admit she was curious. How had he found her? Why was he here? Shaking her head in defeat, she closed her window and padded down the stairs and to the front door. She slipped her feet into Mary's slippers, which often sat near the front door, and carefully opened the front door to find Hunter's imposing frame looming over her.

"Well, hello, my long-lost niece."

"Shh!" She stepped out onto the street but didn't close the door behind her for fear of being locked out.

"What the hell are you doing here?" she repeated.

"Nice to see you too!"

She planted her hands on her hips and raised her eyebrows. She needed answers.

"I wanted to see my lovely niece. Anything wrong with that?"

She crossed her arms. "You've forgiven me, then, for freeing Sam and leaving you to the Fae?"

He sighed. "I don't have anywhere else to go."

So *had* he forgiven her? Or was this supposed to be her chance to make it up to him? She *had* abandoned her uncle and all of his friends in the midst of a massacre while freeing, and running away with, his arch enemy.

She sighed and gritted her teeth. Guilt allowed him in.

"Follow me and keep quiet," she said, rolling her eyes, as she stepped back through the door.

He paused in the entrance hall, gaze sweeping over the carved bannisters, polished wood floors, and the delicate glow of wall lamps. His eyes lingered on the ornate mirrors and the gilt-framed paintings, taking in the quiet opulence that felt a world away from everything he knew.

Ebony took him down to a basement room Mary had once sent her to collect some old silver platters from storage. It was far from any of the sleeping quarters and down so many flights of steps it must have been underground.

As she closed the basement door, darkness closed in around them. She opened the door ajar to give them a little light from the hallway upstairs. It was just enough to see each other's faces.

Hunter gave a low whistle and said, "Well, haven't you got yourself a cushy setup here! An aunt who treats you like a princess!"

"How did you know she's my aunt?"

"You didn't think I knew who the sister of my brother's wife was?"

Ebony took a moment to process that, then her eyes widened, and she instantly regretted taking him in.

"You knew all along that I had a living aunt?" she almost shouted.

"Well, yeah, but I had no idea how accommodating she would be. What could she possibly want from *you* to give you all of this?"

That was it. She'd forgotten how much of an arse he could be.

"Get out," she snapped, pointing at the door.

"Don't you want to know why I'm here?"

"Not if you're going to talk like that about Mary Donahue."

He sighed. "Okay, I'm sorry, I apologise. I was out of line with that comment. I just don't understand how … why … never mind. I need your help."

"You have lied to me countless times, treated me like an idiot, ignored my words of warning. Why would I help you?"

"Because we're family."

"Like that means *anything* to you," she spat.

"Because you left your friends to die at the hands of the Fae, who decimated our camp, by the way, and murdered almost everyone I knew."

"I warned your men not to disrespect them."

"If you had really known that was what could happen, why didn't you shout louder? You either wanted that massacre to happen or you were just as surprised by their malice as we were. You don't know the Fae as well as you think you do."

She scoffed. He didn't know where she'd been for so many months.

"So did you know?" He continued. "You knew they would massacre an entire camp and yet you hardly said a word?"

"Okay! No, I didn't know. They were more violent than I'd ever seen before."

"Why? Why did they do it? No one has heard of the Fae behaving like that before."

Ebony looked away from him.

"You know, don't you?" An awkward silence hung between them. "You know, I've been hearing rumours that I'm not sure I want to believe," he said, eyeing her with suspicion.

Her gust twisted. What had he heard? That the gangs ruled the Dwellings because of her? That she had run from Sam, leaving her friends in danger yet again in the name of self-preservation?

"Rumour has it that Samuel Sanker is possessed by a demon." Her cheeks flushed hot and she shifted her feet uncomfortably. "That he speaks of red eyes and talks to himself. People say he's mad. But you and I know what it is, don't we?" He paused. "Sam is possessed by the Shadow and the Fae came to our camp that night to kill him while he was trapped. And you let him go. You let the Shadow run free, all for your selfish gains."

"I didn't know! I didn't know he was possessed, okay? I needed answers, and you weren't giving them to me."

"How long did it take you to figure it out?"

"Months." She sighed. "He was good to me. The Foryx treated me like an equal, took me in. I had real friends. I … then the Shadow took over and …"

"And you ran again. You ran to your rich aunt's house."

Well, that wasn't quite how the story had played out, but how could she explain that she had crossed over into another realm and discovered her destiny as the Daughter of the Forest? He'd think she'd gone mad.

She nodded.

"And you've found yourself a nice hiding spot here, away from the Shadow, the Jades, and all those you have abandoned."

Her eyes grew glassy as she slowly nodded. He was right. She had abandoned her friends and family, just as he had abandoned her as a child.

"So the least you could do is offer me the same hiding spot."

She looked up at him, surprise evident in her amber eyes.

"I thought you were going to try to persuade me to rejoin the Bounty Hunters and fight the Jades or something."

"It's a bit late for all that. The Bounty Hunters are finished. Gone," Hunter said bitterly, his voice echoing slightly in the cold, dark basement. He paused, swallowing hard before continuing. "And the Jades have taken control of everything. The streets, the markets, the docks — nothing moves without their say. They're ruthless, and they crush anyone who stands in their way."

Ebony's chest tightened. "I know."

Hunter looked up, eyes sharp. "So maybe it's time I was a coward just like you."

She opened her mouth to argue, but nodded in defeat. He was right. She *was* a coward. For all her highwaywoman ways, she'd only ever looked out for herself and had always run at the first sign of danger.

"You'll have to stay down here," she said, "and no one can know. It's already dangerous enough for my aunt to be harbouring one fugitive ..."

He nodded. "Any chance you could find something more comfortable for me to sleep on than a wooden box?" he asked, glancing around the dark basement, which was piled high with storage boxes.

She knew where the maids kept the linen and some thin blankets, but she didn't think he could take a whole duvet set and pillows without it going unnoticed.

"I'll see what I can do." She stepped towards the basement door. "Stay hidden. No one can know you're here or we could both be thrown out. And I have nowhere else to go either."

He nodded, and she closed the door behind her, leaving him in the dark.

What had she got herself into this time?

After scavenging any bedding she could find and delivering it to the basement, she padded back to her room, but there was no way she'd be going back to sleep any time soon.

How was she going to keep this from Mary? How could she lie to the one person who had always been good to her, no matter all she had done? She would need to bring Hunter food and water. She would need to visit him, make sure he was warm enough — all the while being available to her aunt.

She was sure Mary would want to discuss the trip to Henley at length, Ebony's involvement with the Fae, and how this affected the poem and the existence of the Shadow. Not to mention the huge weight that now sat on Ebony's shoulders ... the small matter of uniting city, forest, and Fae ... she didn't want to think about it. How long could she keep her aunt in the dark about why she'd really left Faelynn? About the constant darkness following her?

Ebony lay staring at the wall until she could hear the house waking up around her.

20

The *tick tick* of the grandfather clock in the hall was all that could be heard over breakfast. Each measured beat echoed too loud in Ebony's ears, like a drum in the hush of the grand house. As it chimed the hour, she jumped and stifled nervous laughter.

Her aunt had been different since they had got home — more watchful, almost guarded. Was she still upset about being kept in the dark, about her aunt's true identity? Or perhaps she had picked up on Ebony's new secret. She knew Ebony was hiding something — well, she had an inkling Ebony wasn't telling the full story of the last few months, but she had no idea that Ebony was *literally* hiding something. Or some*one*.

But if Ebony were to tell her the truth — that she had been marked by the Shadow who could burst in at any moment and murder her family again, that the Shadow had begun to infiltrate her mind, Hunter hiding below — Mary would surely throw her out without so much as a backward glance. Mary couldn't risk the life she had built here — her large house, her reputation, her loyal staff … her rebellion.

Ebony was at the bottom of the list of her aunt's priorities, she was sure of it. The woman only wanted her there because of her burning, morbid curiosity regarding the Shadow and the Sister's bizarre poetry.

The room itself pressed on her nerves. Dark green walls lined with oil paintings, polished oak furniture, and a heavy chandelier overhead. Too ornate, too still — nothing moved but the slow sway of candlelight and the twitch of Ebony's restless hands. She longed for open air: wild brambles, the hiss of leaves in the wind, a sky without a ceiling. That green valley they had passed on the way to Henley — so empty, serene, calm. Sometimes the world just felt too overwhelming, and this room was giving her a headache.

She stood abruptly, the chair scraping loud against the polished floor.

"Where are you going?" Mary asked, the first words she'd uttered all morning.

"I— I'll save my breakfast for later," Ebony muttered. "I'm not hungry right now."

She lifted her delicate, flowery, china plate, laden with flaky pastries, and quickly left the room. Once in the corridor, she let out a breath. Guilt nipped at her heels.

My uncle is down there, hungry. What's my purpose in this house anyway? I can't leave, but there's nothing for me to do here. What was she doing playing guest in a gilded cage, when there was so many unresolved questions burning in her mind?

How would she ever be rid of the Shadow's mark? What was it doing to her mind? Was she too late to save herself from its possession?

She headed upstairs, set the plate on the windowsill, and sat heavily on the bed, head in hands. In the dark of night, she could feel the mark burn faintly on her arm. *The Sister said it would claim my mind,* she remembered. And lately … she had woken standing by the window, staring into the night, with no memory of leaving bed. Once, she'd found scratches below the ledge, her name etched into the wood.

And her uncle was sitting in the dark downstairs, hungry, thirsty, and bored … who knew what he was capable of when bored? And what if someone discovered him there?

A sharp knock sounded on her door, and she jumped. Mary stepped into the room, her brow drawn.

"Something is wrong," Mary stated.

"Yeah — something *is* wrong. You're acting … different."

"Am I?"

"Oh, come off it. Ever since we got back, you've acted different, like you don't trust me anymore. Like you're waiting for me to confess something."

"Well, how do I know what else you're keeping from me?"

Ebony swallowed, her throat dry. "How was I supposed to know the Sister and your aunt were the same person?"

Mary's posture eased, but only slightly. "I suppose you couldn't have. But I can't shake the feeling you're still keeping something from me." She paused and sat on the end of the bed. "Are you?"

Ebony looked out the window as a blackbird landed on the ledge and began pecking at a scavenged scrap of bread. Ebony stared at it instead of looking at Mary. "I'm not used to being inside so long. I'm not built for the indoors." A half-truth. She *was* restless, but she was also terrified of what the Shadow might do through her, and she had also grown accustomed to the safety of these walls.

"I know," Mary murmured. "I must remember you're wilder than I ever was."

"I belong in the forest," Ebony admitted. "But I know if I leave this house …" She trailed off, unwilling to say: *The Foryx hate me, the Fae banished me, and the Shadow waits for me in the dark.*

"The Jades, yes," Mary supplied.

"And it's a difficult adjustment for me being here. So … opulent. In Henley …" Ebony looked at the floor, guilt sitting heavy in her chest. "Henley felt like home." At least that wasn't a lie.

"I'm sure we can go back there soon. But for now, there is so much to do. Our movement grows—"

"I know. You're an important, busy woman, doing important, busy work. And I know I can't be involved … too dangerous having that many people see me with my eyes … I just don't have any place in a household like this." She sighed. "Look, don't mind me. I'm being ungrateful and sulky. You go about your day, saving the world one bit at a time, and I'll— I'll be fine."

Mary's expression softened. "We *will* beat the Jades. The streets will be safe again."

"You do know that even if the Snatchers — sorry, the 'Common Custodians'— were still in charge and the Jades had never taken their place, I still wouldn't be able to go into town freely. I'm a street urchin. Underage and belonging to no one."

Mary's expression brightened, as if she'd waited for this. "Ah, yes, that reminds me — I forgot … be back in a moment."

Mary got up and shot out of the room, leaving Ebony bewildered. Moments later, she returned, breathless, and thrust a piece of parchment at her. Ebony took it gingerly — she seemed to be holding a very official-looking document.

"It's your papers. I've registered you to this household. You technically belong to me now — well, this family."

Ebony's hands began to shake, and her vision blurred with tears. Papers. Proof that she *belonged*, that she was a legal, registered citizen of The Dwellings. She had never had real papers like these before. She had fully expected to outgrow the need for them … though she still didn't know her actual age. She could have turned eighteen years ago for all she knew.

"Mary, I …" She looked at her aunt with such a mix of emotions her eyes couldn't make their mind up. Surprise, gratitude, love, guilt … Her aunt had given her so much. and what had she brought her in return? Secrets, threats, and a dishevelled vagabond uncle in her basement. How could she ever repay her?

"I had them drawn up a long time ago, actually — when I discovered you were still alive. I had a vain hope you would

240

find your way to me … or I would find you. I only just found them the other day."

Ebony beamed, a single tear falling down her face. "You beat those damn Jades, you hear me? What I wouldn't give to look a Snatcher in the eyes and prove my innocence!"

"Well, I doubt there will be Custodians again. That initiative failed spectacularly."

Ebony had been the one to help take them down. How tame they seemed now with the Jades ruling the city.

"We'll have to make a new police force that governs all of the Dwellings, not just the Commons." Her aunt smiled at her kindly, knowing how her upbringing in an orphanage had been like a stain she had never been to shift. "Right, well. I need to get on. Places to go, people to see. I'm glad we had this little chat. I was worried …" she paused. "Never mind. It's perfectly understandable that you feel a bit cooped up in this house! But while I work on taking down the Jades, you need to work out how to unite city, forest, and Fae."

"I know," Ebony nodded. She knew all too well and had absolutely no clue where to start.

Mary got to her feet and left Ebony to her thoughts. Her aunt trusted her far too much.

Hunter must be starving, she thought with a pang of guilty.

She quietly got to her feet and took the plate from the windowsill and her glass of water from the bedside table. With the pretence of meandering through the house, breakfast in hand, admiring the art lining every wall, she slowly made her way down the stairs, politely smiling and nodding at the staff as she passed.

At the top of the basement steps, she paused, listening, checking for movement either end of the corridor. Silence.

She hurried down the steep wooden staircase to the basement and opened the closed the door before anyone could see her. She stood in the pitch black, her breath heavy.

And there, in the corner, were the eyes. Red and gleaming — devilish, like flickering flames. Her heart began to race. She was imagining it — she had to be.

"Kill. Slash. Burn," a cold voice rasped.

She froze as the red eyes seemed to drift closer. Her heart began to hammer in her chest and she tried to retreat back through the door, but her legs felt heavy.

"Hunter!" she whispered.

She blinked and the eyes were gone.

"Finally," his voice answered. "I was hoping it was you! I can't see a damn thing in here."

Relief flooded her so hard her knees weakened. She stood still for a moment, straining to see Hunter, or the Shadow, in the darkness. As her heart slowed down, she opened the door slightly — just enough for the light of the house to come in — and gestured for Hunter to be quiet.

Was the Shadow in the room with him or in her mind? It didn't seem like he had heard that voice or seen the eyes. Should she tell him? He had nowhere else to go … was it worth terrifying him?

"Hungry?" she whispered.

"Starving."

"Here," she said, "breakfast."

He almost leapt towards her and grabbed the delicate plate and glass without hesitation. "You call this food? It's all sugar."

"It's all they have at this time of the day. I don't like it much either. I'll try to bring you some dinner later." How, she had no idea.

"Thanks for this," he said between mouthfuls. "I can't stand it down here. All this bloody velvet and sugar up there, and I'm rotting in the dark."

Ebony dropped onto an old sofa, sighing. "I know. Took me a while to get used to it, too." She fell silent, thoughtful.

"What's up?" he asked.

"My aunt gave me some official papers today. I'm officially no longer a street urchin."

"Fat lot of good that will do with the Snatchers out the picture."

"I know, but it's nice to have them at last after so many years of running."

"I suppose that was your doing?"

"What was?"

"Downfall of the Snatchers." Ebony didn't reply. "Didn't I tell you it was a waste of time? There was a power vacuum and worse people took their chance. Predictable, really."

"Yeah, okay, I know — it was a vendetta I was obsessed with, and the Jades are miles worse. I get it, I messed up," Ebony snapped.

Hunter held up his hands in defence. "Nothing we can do about it now."

"That's not true."

"Oh dear, not a new vendetta. So what's your plan this time?"

Ebony clenched her fists. This man was infuriating. "It's not my fight … but there is something happening. The Jades won't last."

"I hope to hell you're right."

"Better than rotting in the dark!" she shot back. "Have you *ever* fought for equality, or do you just avoid conflict at any cost?"

Hunter scoffed. "You're one to talk! At the first sign of danger, you're out of there!"

"Not the same thing. I've fought for equality. Okay, it backfired, but I wasn't afraid of conflict."

"Yes, you like to cause conflict then run from it when it gets too messy."

Ebony scowled. "I'm harbouring you in secret and sneaking you food, and this is how you choose to talk to me?"

"Clearly, no one ever had the guts to be honest to you, Ebony. I'm just showing you who you are."

"Okay, well I'll show who *you* are. You're selfish and arrogant. You only want me around when you need me.

You're disloyal and a rubbish leader. Not much to look up to, to be honest." She wanted to say 'untrustworthy' due to all the secrets he had kept from her, but she could hardly talk. Here she was keeping secrets from her aunt — the only person to ever really care about her.

Hunter gave a barking laugh so loud that Ebony was worried he might be heard. "At last, we speak openly. Anything else you want to say?"

Ebony shot to her feet. "Yeah. Enjoy sitting in the dark all day. You deserve to be alone."

With that, she shut the door behind her and stomped up the stairs, hardly bothering to check if she had been seen by any staff.

The next few days blurred into a cycle of anger, guilt, regret, and a creeping fear she couldn't quite name.

The Shadow in her mind was no longer just a distant threat — it was a creeping presence, gnawing at the edges of her sanity. At night, when the house fell silent and the candle flames flickered low, strange dreams clawed at her sleep and the whispers began: soft, twisting words curling around her thoughts, calling her name like a dark lullaby. Sometimes they urged her toward the window, to unlatch it, to invite the darkness inside.

And the fear of what she might do in those night time wanderings tightened around her chest like iron.

Once, she woke at the window of the drawing room downstairs, hand pressed against the cold glass, breath fogging the pane, with no memory of getting out of bed. What else had she done in her sleep?

Fear stalked her thoughts constantly, and yet she dared not speak of it — not to Mary, not to Hunter. They couldn't know how much danger she had put them in. The Shadow's claws were already sunk deep — and Ebony was afraid she might lose herself to it entirely.

Despite her own worries, she couldn't shake the image of Hunter starving alone in the dark, dank basement. Each day she'd wake feeling sorry for him and would sneak him food, only to have him berate and laugh at her. She'd storm away but the guilt would stubbornly settle in again. And the cycle continued. It wasn't easy stealing food for him every day, though the nights were easiest. She'd wander into the kitchen at dusk, feigning sudden hunger and interest in the chef's stews, slipping a roll or a wedge of cheese into her pocket when backs were turned. Her heart raced each time, convinced the staff were watching, whispering. She was sure rumours of the kitchen thief would start spreading soon.

As a result, Hunter's meals were a bit haphazard. Some fruit, a bread roll, salad — an entire cucumber once. Sometimes he mocked her; sometimes he fell silent, eyes hollow.

The mark on her arm itched more these days, burning faintly in moments of fear — and sometimes, when the house fell silent at night, she could almost hear the Shadow's voice, soft and insidious, tempting her to open the front door and *let it in*.

Rumours of the outside world reached her too: a servant whispering that the Jades had strung up a family in the square for suspected magic. Brutal, shameless, unstoppable.

At breakfast one morning, Mary watched her closely.

"You're sleeping in a lot later these days," she remarked.

Ebony's gut twisted. Mary suspected something.

She had been up late each night, talking with Hunter about the remaining members of the Bounty Hunters. Those who had survived the Fae attack had quickly splintered, and he and Daya had had a fight. She had been offered a job in the city — a low-paid job for the very government they despised. But she'd felt she had no choice. Living in a tent with Hunter and Darrel, they'd had very little between them in the way of resources. One morning, she left and didn't return. The Bounty Hunters had failed — no more vagabonds in the forest. No protection from the city gangs, who began trying to recruit them.

Ebony had pointed out that The Foryx were alive and strong — vagabonds with a cause. But Hunter had always sworn against them and wouldn't listen to Ebony's insistence that they were good people.

Ebony looked up at Mary and shrugged. "Bad dreams," she lied, stomach tight.

Bad dreams? More like the burning world of the Shadow realm, sleepwalking, voices, the Shadow calling me.

Every night, she was infuriatingly close to the Mother only to lose sight of her, just before the world went dark and the red eyes glared at her, and a cold, shrill voice called her name.

Spending time with Hunter late into the night helped her avoid those nighttime wanderings … and although they were in the dark, the perfect place for the Shadow to find them, she didn't feel so much fear with Hunter there. If it made an appearance, they would face it together.

Mary gave her an understanding smile as if to say, 'Sorry you're still trapped inside all the time but it's for the best.'

"I've been busy with the movement," Mary explained. "But I need your help today. Let's go over the poem again."

"Again?" Ebony rolled her eyes. "We've picked it out word by word," Ebony protested, but a growing sense of fear burned.

"The shadows rise, Ebony. We're running out of time. We need a plan. We need to work out how to unite city, forest, and Fae."

Hunter had been a welcome distraction, but Ebony knew she had been ignoring the Sister's words. It was just all too much … too much to wrap her head around. Too much expectation. Too much danger.

"Okay, fine," Ebony snapped, if only just to get her aunt off her back. "We'll go over it in a bit."

Carrying a plate of pastries as if to take them upstairs, she fled to the hallway and tiptoed towards the basement. She scurried down the steps to the basement and quickly shut the door behind her.

"Hunter?" she whispered.

"Ebony?"

"I've brought some food, but I can't stay long."

He sighed. "I thought as much. A maid came down here

earlier with a candle and glanced about ... then she just left."

Ebony swore under her breath. "She didn't see you, did she?"

"No, it was too dark. But it was close."

Ebony sighed. "Someone must have seen me come down here. I don't know how much longer you can stay here, Hunter, it's getting risky ..." She paused. "I have to go. My aunt needs my help with something ..."

She hadn't shared their revelations with Hunter. Something told her he wouldn't believe a word of it.

She felt for his hand and handed him the pastries, then closed the door softly behind her. She tiptoed up the wooden steps and—

"What were you doing down there?" a voice asked.

Ebony almost jumped out of her skin. Her aunt was standing in front of her, hands on hips, her eyebrows raised. Ebony's heart raced, but she held her aunt's stern gaze. If she looked away, she knew she would look guilty. Her mind whirred.

Think.

"Just wondering what was down there," she said. "Nothing but dusty boxes. I can see why no one goes down there."

"We could clear it out for you, give you your own study. Happy to go down there now and see what we can do." Mary narrowed her eyes.

"No! No. No need for that. You're right — we need to talk about the poem, the plan. Let's go to the library and riddle it out."

Mary looked torn between exploring the basement for Ebony's secrets and working on the poem that had dominated her thoughts for more than a year now.

She sighed. "Glad to hear you're ready to face reality." She beckoned Ebony to follow.

As they walked away, irony dawned on Ebony. Once, Hunter had been the one to protect her by keeping her in a tent ... much good that had done. Now, the roles had reversed. She hoped against hope that he was never discovered. Mary would never trust her again.

21

"So what's the plan then?" Mary asked, as if Ebony had all the answers to the world's problems written on the palm of her hand. She closed the library door and walked further into the room before turning to face her niece.

"I don't have a plan. Uniting city, forest, and Fae isn't possible. They all hate each other."

"So the shadows win and we all get sucked into a never-ending world of darkness?"

"Well, that *would* be bad. But I'm not a hero. I'm not some great leader. I run from danger — I don't fight it."

"My dear, from what I've seen and heard, you *are* danger."

Ebony had to laugh at that. "Colour-changing eyes and skill with a dagger won't do anything against the shadows."

"But your ring will. The poem established that. Well, it's *my* ring, really—"

"I'm pretty sure it was your sister's ring, so it should have been handed down to me, her daughter."

"Well, alright. But I think the universe led you to it. If you hadn't looted our cart—"

"Again, sorry about that—"

"You really do need to stop apologising, my dear. I got over it a long time ago." She paused and gave Ebony one of her stern looks. "So, the ring. The poem says, *'To open and seal the tearing night, the ring is the key to turn'*. So the ring is the key to the Shadowlands ... somehow."

"From what I've seen of the Shadow Door, I have no clue how this ring could open it ... but I guess I never tried anything ... I wasn't stupid enough to attempt it."

Though there had been that one time when the door had almost sucked her in. The Fae had blamed it on the Shadow's mark, but had that been to do with the ring?

"So we've got the key," Mary continued, "we just need to find a way of uniting everyone."

"But why? What has the city and forest got to do with it?"

Mary was stumped, and she shrugged. "The poem doesn't say."

"Maybe it *isn't* finished? Maybe we have to wait for another stanza?"

"Or maybe you are stalling for time. Maybe we need to

just get on with it and all the unknowns will start to fall into place?"

"And what's your role in all of this? You send your niece off to battle with the deadliest creatures known to the world, and then what? Stand by and see what happens next?"

Mary looked deeply offended and dropped down into a nearby chair.

"I'm sorry," Ebony began. "That was unfair, I—"

"I know that's what it looks like, but I'm fighting my own war. And all this week I've been preparing the rebellion, training them for battle. The poem says *'gather strength and forge the light'*. My people are learning to fight with burning swords and arrows. Fight fire with fire, I say."

Ebony's jaw dropped. While she had been secretly harbouring a fugitive in her aunt's face and lying to her face, Mary Donahue had been building an army of city-dwellers. She was already doing her part towards uniting city, forest, and Fae.

"I think *'forge the light'* is to do with the Fae. They emit lightning from their staves. The shadows fear it."

"Well then, we need to get them to join the fight."

Easier said than done, Ebony thought.

"Well, if you have an idea for how to get archenemies to work together to fight a darkness they have never encountered, then I'm all ears!"

"Well, actually—"

A scream rang through the house. Mary jumped up and wrenched open the library door. Daisy came tearing along the corridor, terror in her eyes.

"What's wrong?" Mary asked.

"D-dark as n-night," the maid stammered. "R-Red eyes like flame ..."

Ebony's head dropped into her chest, her stomach twisted, and her eyes turned red.

The maid looked at her with horror and pointed. "Like that," she said.

Mary turned to see Ebony backing into the library — as far from the maid, the door, the danger as she could get.

It had come for her.

"Where?" she managed to say, but it came out as a croaked whisper.

"In the stairway down to the basement."

Ebony's eyes grew wide and her hands began to shake.

Hunter. Hunter was trapped, alone, and unprotected.

"Daisy, show me where you saw it," Mary said, her voice surprisingly calm.

"Are you crazy?" Ebony yelled. "It will kill you!"

The maid began shaking, looking from Mary to Ebony and back again, clearly debating who she should listen to.

"I need to see it again. Know that it's real."

"It's not just a story, Mary!" Ebony shouted. "It's not a thing to marvel at — it's a thing to run from!"

"If you can't be the hero, then I will," Mary snapped. "Someone has to face to up to it!"

"You're a fool, Mary. Your obsession is driving you to danger. To madness."

"You stay here, Daisy. I'll go myself."

"No!" Ebony yelled as her aunt left her sight.

She knew she had to do *some*thing — *anything*. Both her remaining family members were in danger because of her — because of this damn mark on her arm. But fear rooted her to the spot, like every cell in her body was paralyzed.

"FIRE!" she heard her aunt yell.

And the world descended into chaos.

Ebony's feet acted of their own volition, racing towards the basement, towards the fire. Towards the Shadow. She had to get Hunter out just as he had once done for her.

Servants rushed past her, and the world grew blurry as she raced down the hallways towards the smoke. Towards licking flame. Towards death and destruction. Towards her greatest fears.

Her feet carried her down the basement steps, which were lined with flames. She hardly noticed her aunt pulling at her clothes to stop her. But Mary didn't know who was down there.

"Hunter!" Ebony yelled and burst into the basement, which was alight with flame. She coughed through the smoke and saw him curled up in a corner, cowering from the fire.

"Hunter!" she cried. She would *not* lose another family member.

A wooden beam had fallen from the ceiling and was alight, trapping Hunter behind it. Ebony leapt over one end like the flame wasn't there at all and heaved her uncle to his feet. She pushed him forwards, and he toppled face-first over the beam, collapsing in a coughing fit on the other side.

In the doorway, a dark figure formed. A figure with bright red eyes and claws like tendrils of smoke. The Shadow. Its very presence turned the air colder, even as flames crackled and roared around them. They would never get past it. They were trapped in a burning room underground, the Shadow between them and the door.

Ebony froze. The mark on her arm burned, so hot it felt like molten iron branding her flesh.

Stop.

The command wasn't spoken aloud, but she heard it all the same — a whisper curling through her mind, slick and cold as oil.

Stay where you are. Let him burn.

She felt her limbs stiffen, her muscles locking under invisible chains. Smoke stung her eyes, tears streaming down her cheeks, but her feet wouldn't move. Hunter was crawling toward the door, dragging himself through the cinders — and she couldn't help him.

The Shadow drifted closer, its red eyes gleaming like coals. Ebony could feel its will pressing against hers, worming into her thoughts, cold fingers curling around her heart.

Let go, it hissed. *Leave him.*

The fire roared higher, licking at the walls, swallowing the dry wood with a hiss and a hungry crackle. Fear clawed up her throat, raw and feral. Her chest heaved; the room blurred. She could almost feel the old terror of fire in her bones: the searing heat, the smoke stealing her breath, the memory of flames burning down her orphanage, her best friend inside.

Abandon him, run from this chaos, like you always do, the Shadow coaxed.

For a heartbeat, her body obeyed. She stepped towards the door, towards the Shadow, her legs moving of their own accord, heart pounding, shame curdling in her gut. The mark on her arm pulsed, the Shadow's laughter echoing inside her skull.

But through the rising smoke, she saw Hunter, broken and gasping, trying to reach the door. She saw the terror in his eyes as she ignored his desperate pleas.

All her life, she had fled from fear. She had fled every time she had brought danger to those she was close to. But this time, running meant losing everything: her family, her freedom — herself.

"No," she whispered, her voice hoarse.

The Shadow's claws coiled tighter in her mind, but she

clenched her jaw, forcing her gaze to stay on the thing she feared most: the black figure, the flames.

The heat scorched her skin; the smoke raked her lungs. Terror clawed at her ribs, begging her to flee — but she stayed. She faced it.

The mark burned like wildfire now, white-hot agony searing through her arm.

"I said, NO!"

With a cry, she tore free. The Shadow's grip slipped, just for a breath — but it was enough.

The Shadow shrieked, a sound of rage and disbelief, as its hold on her mind shattered.

Ebony lunged forward, seizing Hunter by the shoulders. For the first time, Ebony wasn't running from the chaos.

The blue ring on her finger blazed to life — a sudden, blinding flare of blue that pierced the smoke and shadow alike. For a heartbeat, the basement glowed with its cold, fierce brilliance, cutting through the red glow of fire and the darkness that clung to the walls. It pulsed once, twice — each beat pushing the Shadow back. Its smoky claws curled away, its shape breaking and twisting as if the light scalded it.

The Shadow let out another shriek, higher and rawer, and

fled, streaming like black smoke up the stairway, clawing at the walls as it went. For a heartbeat, its red eyes met hers, but the blue light flared brighter, and the eyes vanished into the darkness.

Ebony heaved Hunter to his feet, dragging him to the open door, which was now a ball of flame. Behind them, the basement was devoured by fire, the orange light twisting through the smoke like a living thing. Hunter coughed, gasping for breath, and Ebony's chest burned from the heat — but her mind was her own again.

She pulled Hunter up the burning stairs and was greeted with a man's hand as they emerged from the flames.

The whole hallway was alight now.

With a questioning glance at Hunter, the servant led them towards the front door.

"I'm not leaving without her!" Ebony heard Mary shriek from outside.

"She's here! I've got her!" the servant yelled.

"Oh, thank the Gods!" Mary cried, tears streaming down her ash-strewn cheeks.

"What? Who?" she spluttered as they were thrust out the front door and onto the streets. "Huntington Sparrow?"

She looked at Ebony with bewilderment and back to the man now crouched on her front doorsteps, coughing up ash.

"How? When? How was he ..." she pointed inside the burning house.

But Ebony wasn't listening. She sat next to her uncle and put an arm around his shoulders. "You're safe now. We're out."

She had done it. She had faced her fear of fire. She had run into danger. She had ignored all self-preservation and saved someone else for a change. *She* had been the hero!

A weight lifted from her chest and her wrist began to burn. She pulled up her sleeve to reveal the Shadow's red mark — burning bright like embers in a fire.

"What is that on your arm?" Mary shrieked.

And then it was gone. The long finger marks, the burn in her flesh. Gone. Like it had never been there.

Had she just got rid of the Shadow's mark by facing her deepest fears?

"What is going on?" her aunt yelled. Mary roughly pulled her to her feet. "What in Atlaan's name was Huntington Sparrow doing in my house?" she yelled over the crackling of the burning building. The entire house was alight.

"I— he— he needed my help …" Ebony said weakly.

"My lady, we have to go—" a servant said, touching her shoulder. But she brushed him off.

"How long have you been keeping this from me, hiding him in my basement?" Mary snapped, grabbing onto Ebony's collar.

"Since we got back from Henley."

Mary's jaw dropped. "After all I've done for you … how could you? … Do you know who this man is?"

"He's my uncle."

"And a wanted criminal!"

"So am I!" Ebony bit back. She could feel the heat of the fire on her back now.

"Please … it's my fault," Hunter said in between splutters. "I made her take me in."

Mary scowled. "The last time I saw this man, I told him in no uncertain terms that I never wanted to see him again!"

"Please, Mary—" Hunter said, getting to his feet.

Mary let out a blood-curdling shriek and pointed behind Hunter into the burning house. They all turned to stare at the red-eyed shadow standing at the edge of its wreck and ruin, framed by the flaming doorway.

"Ebony Wick," its cruel voice rasped, and it swiped its clawed shadow hand through the air.

A large gash sliced through Hunter's abdomen, and he collapsed.

"No!" Ebony yelled. It reached its arm up again, its gaze locked on Mary. "Not my aunt, you bastard!" Ebony yelled and reached her ringed hand outwards. Again, light burst from it, but this time, it shot through the heart of the Shadow, and it shattered like glass.

The world stood still for a moment before Ebony's knees gave way and she fell beside her uncle. She cradled him in her lap, but she was too late. The light had already left his eyes.

"Are you happy?" she yelled over her shoulder. "Now you never will have to see him again!"

"My lady, we must go!"

Mary grabbed Ebony's shoulder. "Ebony, the Jades are here."

Tears streamed down Ebony's cheeks. "I don't care! I'm not leaving him!"

"Ebony …"

"Go! Run!" Ebony shrieked.

And she watched as her aunt and her servant fled their burning house, and the oncoming force of Jades storming down the street.

Ebony felt herself being torn from her uncle's lifeless body, and her hands were bound behind her back with rope.

"Ebony Wick. We've got you at last," a cruel voice rasped in her ear.

22

A rough burlap sack was shoved over Ebony's head, the scratchy weave pressing against her cheeks and tangling in her hair. The sour stench of old hay, sweat, and cow dung filled her nostrils, making her gag. Before she could draw breath to scream, two large hands clamped onto her arms, their grip bruising, unyielding.

Kicking and screaming, she fought for her freedom, to no avail. Her boots scraped helplessly over the cobbles, the stones uneven beneath her feet. They dragged her forward, each jerking step rattling her teeth. The coarse fabric chafed at her skin, heat prickling on her scalp as panic surged in her chest. She could barely breathe; the bag clung to her mouth with every gasp, trapping her own warm breath inside. Sweat trickled from her brow, stinging her eyes as she struggled.

Her pulse roared in her ears, drowning out the muted sounds of the city beyond the sack. Somewhere in the distance, she could hear the rumble of cart wheels and the bark of traders, but it all felt far away, unreachable behind the darkness pressed to her face. Twisting, she tried to turn her head, to guess where they were, but it was hopeless.

"Where are you taking me?" she demanded, but the words came out hoarse and shaky. No reply — only the slap of boots against stone and the scrape of something metal.

The ground seemed to slope downhill, then level out. At one point, they stopped abruptly, and she heard muttered words exchanged above her head — too low and fast to catch.

Her captors moved again, jerking her forward, and her shoulder slammed painfully into a stone wall. Ebony gasped, biting back a cry. Her knees buckled, but the men dragged her upright, one hand knotting painfully into her hair through the sack, forcing her to stumble on.

She tried to count her steps, to mark each corner they turned, but fear fogged her mind, turning minutes into a shapeless stretch of breathless panic. She no longer knew where in the city she was, or even which way she faced.

The men stopped again. She heard the slow scrape of a heavy key turning in a lock, then the groan of iron hinges stiff with rust.

They shoved her forward. She stumbled, knees striking stone, pain shooting up her thighs. Cold, damp air rose around her, smelling of mould, smoke, and something sour. At last, rough hands yanked the sack from her head. Light stabbed her eyes, forcing them to squint.

She was locked in a cage, surrounded by rusted metal bars — but it wasn't what she'd expected a jail to look like. She wasn't in a long corridor of multiple cells, but in the centre of a mess hall, which was a hive of activity. She wasn't to be hidden away in some dark, forgotten cell but jeered at and taunted like a caged animal.

The Jades were bigger than ever before — an entire army of cruel faces pointing at her and grimacing as they ate.

"What's wrong with her eyes?" one man said loudly enough for the whole room to hear.

"Diseased, probably. She's just a dirty urchin."

"Men," a voice bellowed, and the whole room fell silent and turned to a wiry-looking man with beady eyes. Ebony assumed this was the new leader of The Black Jades, though he was not what she'd expected. They normally respected brawn over brains. "This is no mere street urchin," the man continued. "This," he pointed directly at her from across the room as she nursed a throbbing knee, "is Ebony Wick, betrayer of The Jades, Demon of the Forest, murderer, liar, and thief."

A collective gasp ran through the room as he strode towards the cell, and all eyes turned to her. So, her reputation proceeded her.

"She thought she could cheat us. Break her word. Slip between the cracks. But at last, the red-eyed witch is where she belongs — outwitted, outmatched."

Outwitted? Outmatched? She had been ambushed outside her burning house!

"The Demon of the Forest is no more. We no longer need to fear Rundlewood Forest. We can take it for ourselves."

Had they feared the forest because of *her*? Because of rumours about her red eyes and supposed magic? A brittle laugh escaped Ebony — she couldn't help it. Such ignorant fools, blind to what truly lurked beyond the treeline.

"Speak, Demon," the tall man barked.

Ebony swallowed, her heart pounding. Think. She had no dagger, no bow, no allies — just words.

"If you think you can win against the Fae," she began, her voice tight with scorn, "then be my guest. Wander freely into the forest and start a war with the deadliest of creatures—"

"You think fairies scare us?" he cut her off, laughing, and the room laughed with him. But one pair of eyes stayed solemn, fixed on Ebony from the far side of the room.

"You don't know what you're up against," she murmured,

half to herself, half to them. They had no idea what true danger waited in the trees — or what the Fae would do to invaders.

The memory of the Fae massacring the Bounty Hunters caught in her throat. She hesitated. If the Fae killed the Jades, she might never leave this cage — who'd be left to drag her out? But ... if she could *guide* them, coax them into moving on the Fae while keeping herself alive, then maybe ...

A dangerous idea sparked. Slowly, carefully, she let the words slip out.

"But who am I to stop you? Go ahead. Annihilate your entire gang." She laughed darkly. "Risk your lives, if you want ... but without my help, you'll be as good as dead."

A ripple of uncertainty crossed a few faces. She caught the leader's gaze, steady and cold, and raised her eyebrows, waiting for a response.

"Without your help? What can a lowly urchin do to help The Black Jades!" He said 'The Jades' like they were some long-standing royalty, with a history of greatness.

"How do you think I survived alone in the woods all those years? How do you think I got my demon powers? These red eyes?"

To her surprise, the room seemed to actually be listening to her — believing her, even. Inside, her pulse thundered.

What are you doing, Ebony?

But it was too late to stop. A plan was forming — still fragile, foolish, dangerous — but it was the only plan she had.

"Don't you think the Fae and the Demon are connected?" she continued, forcing steel into her voice. "How else did a lowly urchin destroy the Snatchers and the Bounty Hunters? You don't really think I did that alone?"

"So it's true? You *are* the cause of Hunter Sparrow's demise?"

For a breath, the voices around her blurred into silence. The words stabbed deep, sharp as any blade. Hunter's lined face flickered through her mind — the haunted look in his eyes as the Shadow stood before them before slicing him in two. Her heart twisted in her chest, but if they saw even a flicker of grief, it would be over. They'd know she was lying.

She swallowed hard, forcing the rising tears back down her throat until it burned, burying the memories of her uncle at the back of her mind.

"It's true," she said in the coldest tone she could muster. "And just before you captured me, I finished the job. Hunter Sparrow is dead."

The lie tasted like dirt. Guilt clawed at her ribs, hot and merciless, but she made herself look them in the eye.

She paused to take a deep breath and calm her erratic heart and twisted her mouth into a cruel grimace. "I set that house ablaze," she said, loud and clear, forcing venom into the words that made her stomach roil, "with Hunter Sparrow inside."

Inside, her heart howled with grief and self-loathing. But she forced her shoulders back, raising her chin, hiding the shaking deep beneath her skin.

"How?" the leader said, disbelievingly. But she could see the fear in his eyes. If she could do that to a house, to an old friend, what more was she capable of?

Ebony let the question hang in the smoky air, her silence deliberate, heavy. Slowly, she lifted her gaze, her eyes burning a bright red, eying every man and woman in the room like they were meat.

"I'm the Demon in the Woods."

The words weren't shouted. They didn't need to be. She let them settle, heavy as iron, her stare cold and unwavering — as though that single, simple truth explained everything.

She was sure she didn't imagine the entire room leaning

away from her as she grinned at them with the wildest expression she could muster. These people were so afraid of the unknown that she could weave any supernatural tale and they'd believe her.

"M-maybe we should put her somewhere more secure …" a quiet voice said from the back of the room.

"No. If she really is capable of all that, then she can show us her powers right here, right now," the leader snapped with a wicked grin.

"It doesn't work like that," Ebony said, making it clear she thought the man an idiot. "I work with the Fae. Without them, I'm just an urchin." She gave a careless shrug, the red of her eyes glinting in the torchlight. "But *with* them … there are no limits. You've seen what happened to the Snatchers. To the Bounty Hunters. You'd get rid of The Foryx, that's for sure. And I'd be only too happy to help," she lied. She was almost enjoying this vindictive character she'd created for herself.

Another deliberate pause. She let them imagine it: the Jades stepping into more power, feared not only by the city dwellers, but by the very monsters that haunted the forest.

Her tone hardened. "But if you go to them without me — try to bargain, threaten, or so much as breathe the wrong word …" Her gaze swept the room, settling on each doubtful face in turn. "You'd be dead before dawn."

The leader took a moment to think as heads turned from him to Ebony and back again.

"You will stay in this cell so we can monitor you. You are no threat without the Fae. We will discuss what is to be done with you."

With that, he turned on his heel and left the room, and the hall filled with chatter. Each time a pair of eyes turned towards her, she glared at them and grinned maniacally. These brawny men were afraid of her *eyes*. They could easily kill her at a moment's notice, so vulnerable in that cell in the centre of the room, yet their superstitions held them back. It was sheer stupidity — but it was all she had right now to keep her alive and with a chance of escape. Besides, she had bigger worries. The Shadows were on the move.

Slowly, the room emptied as The Jades were called for their various duties. Only one person remained; her guard, she presumed.

Ebony stood on a hillside in that familiar, endless grey, but the streets of the burning city below were eerily still. No whispering shapes, no flickers of red-eyed malice in the fog. Only silence so deep it pressed against her eardrums, making her heartbeat sound thunderous in her own chest.

She turned slowly, bare feet sinking into ash that stained her toes black, and wondered where the Shadows had gone.

But then, on the far horizon, she saw it: a single line of darkness, like billowing, black smoke, twisting and crawling up a barren hillside towards the Shadow Door. No faces, no claws — just a tide of darkness.

And though it moved silently, Ebony felt its hunger. They were gathering. They had almost reached the breach into her world.

"No," she whispered, her voice lost in the ash-choked air. Raw fear coiled in her gut. "Help us! Come out of hiding and help!" she yelled at the top of her lungs, hoping against hope that the Mother could hear her.

A cold tremor raced through her as the line of shadow began to swell, to split and unfurl, becoming thousands of drifting coils rising up the hillside. The Shadow Door shimmered at the summit, pale and beckoning.

Her eyes flew open, her heart hammering in her chest. The smell of urine, sweat, and rusted iron flooded her senses. She was still in the cage, ribs aching, breath shallow.

The Shadows were on the move.

Her guard approached her; a burly woman with blonde hair plaited tightly down the back of her head. She wore leather armour and carried a large sword on her hip. Her eyes a burning red, Ebony snarled at her and forced her aching limbs to sit upright.

"Ebony Wick," the guard whispered.

"That's me," Ebony replied, her voice echoing across the empty hall.

"Shh!" The woman's eyes widened, and she gestured for Ebony to keep her voice down. "I'm with The Foryx, I'm a spy. My name is Astrid."

Ebony gasped and her eyes turned purple. So she might actually have a friend in this place!

"All that stuff I said earlier about destroying The Foryx ..."

"Ebony. You are *not* the Demon in the Woods, you did not destroy the Bounty Hunters, and you are not in league with the Fae. I know you're no threat the The Foryx."

"But I don't even *want* to harm The Foryx. I'm just trying to find a way out of here. And, by the way ... I sort of am in league with the Fae ..."

Astrid looked at her disbelievingly.

"How is Sam?" Ebony asked, doing her best to show how much she truly cared.

Astrid's expression darkened. "Since you abandoned him, you mean?" Ebony didn't respond, her gut twisting uncomfortably. "He is very sick. The Demon has left him … and his life force seems almost drained."

For a heartbeat, relief pulsed through Ebony so strong it stole her breath. *So that's what could have happened to me …* She had felt the Shadow in her mind — heard its whispers, nearly lost herself to its will — but she hadn't carried it as long as Sam had.

She swallowed hard, forcing the words out, voice low but urgent. "You have to warn them all, Astrid. The Shadows are on the move. They're coming."

Astrid's brow furrowed sharply, a muscle ticking in her jaw. "Shadows? There's more than one?" she whispered.

"Thousands," Ebony hissed. "A whole realm of them, and they are breaking through to our world."

Astrid's eyes widened, the blood draining from her freckled face. Her gaze darted around the hall, as if she half-expected dark shapes to slither out from the corners that very moment.

"So … we could all end up like Sam?" she murmured, her voice cracking. She gripped the bars of the cell, knuckles whitening, her breath quickening.

"Sam had it lucky," Ebony said, her own voice hollow. "He was used, then left — most people will simply be killed."

Astrid's shoulders stiffened, the leather of her armour creaking as she swallowed hard, trying to keep her composure. "But what— what do we do?" she pressed, the words tumbling out in a desperate rush.

Ebony shrugged helplessly. "The Shadows don't like the light. They thrive in darkness and fire."

Astrid looked back at Ebony, eyes brimming with questions she couldn't quite form as the weight of what she'd just heard settled between them.

Ebony knew what *she* had to do — close the door — but she had no idea how. But first she had to enter the Shadowlands through the door … she tried not to think about it.

"Not much *I* can do from this cell," Ebony stated. "Please warn The Foryx. The Fae are our only hope now."

"There's no chance the Fae will work with The Foryx," Astrid replied. "Not without …"

279

"Not without someone who knows how to deal with them both? Someone like me?"

Astrid nodded slowly, comprehension dawning in her eyes. "If I set you free, my position here will be compromised ..."

"If you don't, we could all die at the hands of the shadows."

"What do we do once you're free?"

"We go to The Foryx and then find the Fae Door."

"The what?"

"The door to their realm — it's where I went when I left."

"And what if ... what if you don't make it out and can't show us how to find it?"

"Head west of the wooden village, look for a single archway in the forest. No wall holding it up, just an archway in a clearing."

"Nothing more specific than that?"

"I found it by accident," Ebony admitted.

"So we head west and hope for the best?"

Ebony nodded.

Astrid swallowed heavily. "We both need to get out of here, then," she declared, and Ebony felt relief flood through her. "I'll be back soon." She strode out of the hall, and Ebony took a deep breath, leaning against the uncomfortable bars of the cell. But she hardly had a moment to think before the Jade leader and three others marched towards her with purpose.

"You will take us to the Fae and negotiate with them. Together, we will take down The Foryx and share the forest with the Fae. If you are lying about anything you have told us, we will slit your throat without hesitation."

Ebony saw Astrid return to the hall through a far door, carrying a sack of what looked to be her worldly goods. Ebony's eyes widened, and she glared at her and gave an infinitesimal shake of her head. Astrid slowly backed out of the room before any of the leaders could see her.

"Well?" the leader prompted. "We could just kill you now and be done with it."

"I was just thinking about what I might say to the Fae King to persuade him to fight for our cause."

"*Our* cause?"

"I want The Foryx gone as much as you do."

The leader furrowed his brows. "Why? You were close with them once."

"They abandoned me to die when we took down the Snatchers," she lied. "They betrayed me."

"You do know this doesn't guarantee your freedom."

Ebony pursed her lips and raised her eyebrows. "When do we leave?"

"As soon as you tell us exactly where it is we're going."

He glared at her expectantly. Ebony's chest twisted, and she refrained from gulping. She didn't have long to form the next part of her plan.

"We need to go to the Fae Door. It's in the middle of Rundlewood Forest and not easy to find. But I know where it is." *Sort of.* She hoped she would be able to find it again.

"Where's your guard?" one of the men snapped.

"Stepped out briefly to, uh, relieve myself, chief," Astrid replied, striding into the hall, her sack nowhere to be seen.

"We told you not to leave her side."

"Sorry, it was an emergency. Won't happen again."

The men eyed her but turned to the leader as he strode away.

"I look forward to killing you myself when we discover your lies, Ebony Wick," the leader said over his shoulder as he left the room.

Hopefully he wouldn't get the chance.

23

It was bright but damp outside as Ebony was dragged from her cell and out of the Jade's headquarters, a looming fortress of stained stone and rusted bars, once an old prison. The iron gates clanged shut behind her, and as she blinked away the light, she realised with a jolt that she knew this place. She and Sam had helped liberate it only a few months ago.

Around her, the Jades gathered in force. Dozens of them, maybe more: hard-eyed men and women in mismatched leather and patched coats. Some were armed with daggers and cudgels, others with swords or rusted axes. Ebony caught glimpses of faces she vaguely recognised from back alleys and market corners — smugglers, brawlers, black-market traders, cutthroats she'd once traded with.

Cold iron cuffs bit into her wrists, too tight, cutting off the blood flow until her fingers tingled. Hands pushed and shoved her forward, almost making her stumble as her feet splashed through rain-filled potholes and slick puddles. All around her rose the noise of the city waking: market criers, haggling voices, cart wheels grinding over cobbles — yet the crowd of Jades parted those streets like a blade through cloth, and no one dared stand in their way.

They marched over the old stone bridge spanning the river — one she had crossed countless times before, pockets heavy with well-earned coins or contraband meant for the black market. But today, she walked almost empty-handed, surrounded on all sides by the very people she had once betrayed. They didn't need to know about the dagger in her boot.

Ahead, the forest waited, and behind her, an army of Jade enforcers — far too many to count now — tramped through the mud with grim, eager faces, ready for a fight they could not possibly win.

Eventually, they reached the treeline of Rundlewood Forest. Ebony paused, heart hammering against her ribs like a caged bird. The air smelled of damp earth and rotting leaves — familiar, almost comforting, yet it filled her with dread all the same.

When a Jade prodded her roughly between the shoulder blades, she stood firm, masking her fear with annoyance.

"You expect me to go into the woods handcuffed?"

"Can't have you doin' a runner."

"I told your leader — we're on the same side. Besides, I'll trip every thirty seconds. It will take forever to find the Fae Door! And what if we're attacked? Don't you want the demon in the woods on your side?"

"I'll remove your cuffs if you shut up."

"Deal."

With a clink of metal, her wrists felt lighter, and she straightened her arms before her, grateful for the chance to stretch her aching muscles.

"Lead the way, then."

She turned toward the forest, but her feet hesitated.

She was gambling everything on a lie. She had told the Jades she could guide them to the Fae, speak for them, convince them to parley. But the truth gnawed at her insides: she didn't know how to find the door. She didn't know if the Fae would even answer her call. And if she failed, the Jades would not hesitate to slit her throat and leave her body to rot among the brambles.

And if she succeeded … she would watch them march to their slaughter. She could almost taste the blood on the air already.

She contemplated her options. She could try to run, but

with so many of the Jades around her, it was unlikely she would escape with her life. So she did as she was told, making a meal of the undergrowth, about fifty percent sure she was heading in the wrong direction to buy herself time. She wasn't entirely sure she'd be able to find the Fae Door again. And if she did, what would she say to them? "Hi, I know you hate me, but would you mind forging an alliance with a gang of people you hate even more? Thanks."

This is madness, she thought, swallowing hard.

She needed time to strategise, and The Jades would never know she was straying off the path on purpose.

Rain began to fall through the treetops, fine at first, then steadily heavier, drumming on leaves and running cold rivulets down Ebony's neck. Around her, at least thirty or forty Jades trudged grimly through the mire, their boots sinking into moss and mud. Some cursed under their breath; others swatted at brambles that tore at their cloaks and sleeves. The damp made their leather armour squeak and creak with every step, and the smell of wet earth mixed with the stink of sweat and unwashed bodies.

They moved together, not as an army but as a dangerous tide, blades and cudgels hidden beneath dark cloaks, eyes darting warily at every sudden sound. Occasionally, a voice rose in complaint — about the mud, the rain, the cold — but each time it was hushed quickly by a sharper voice.

Ebony felt their presence pressing close behind her, heavy as a threat. If they realised how lost she truly was, she wouldn't make it to the next clearing alive.

She kept her head low, trying to hide the flicker of worry in her gaze. She could only hope Astrid had managed to slip away unseen, to carry word back to The Foryx. And she prayed to the Mother that they could actually find the door. At this rate they were as likely to find it as she was.

"Where exactly are you taking us?" one of the men growled, his voice rough with suspicion.

"To meet the Fae."

"And where is that exactly?"

Ebony had to refrain from laughing. That was the exact same question she had been asking herself.

"I'm taking you to the Fae Door — the entrance to their realm."

"They have their own realm?" a female voice asked — a girl not too dissimilar to Ebony, though lacking the distinct red eyes.

The men looked at her as if to say, 'Why do you care? We are Jades — we don't ask questions like that.'

The girl shrugged and looked away.

"I swear we've been going round in circles …" one man remarked.

Ebony swore under her breath. They were starting to cotton on to the fact that she had been buying herself time to think what she was going to say to King Alvero. So far, she'd come up with nothing. She'd just have to turn up at the door and wing it. Time to stop stalling to head in the right direction and actually attempt to find the Fae. She sighed and turned, scanning the sea of muddy, rain-soaked figures.

The men trudged around her in a loose circle, their breath steaming in the cold air. Then, parting the line of men like a prow cutting through water, the leader stepped forward, his coat slick with rain, his hair plastered to his brow.

She felt the weight of his gaze before she saw him. His boots squelched through the mud as he pushed past two men and came to stand in front of her, close enough that she caught the scent of wet wool and smoke.

"If you're lying, Wick …" he growled, his voice low and dangerous, barely rising over the hiss of rain on leaves.

"I know — you'll cut my throat and leave me to rot. Look, Rundlewood Forest is a big place, and if you don't know it well it can all look very similar. But I know it like the back of my hand. I know where I'm going." It was almost true …

She felt herself walking with more purpose and began heading in the right direction, judged by the angle of the sun through the treetops. The wooden village was to the south and the Fae Door somewhere west of that. She would need to retrace her steps through woodland had once blundered through in a blind panic, while avoiding the wooden village. She just needed *something* she recognised.

At long last, she spied a burned wooden barn through the trees. She knew exactly where she was. Memories surfaced of being tied to a post, surrounded by flame, hearing the Shadow's violence outside … she veered off to the west, an army of Jades trampling through the undergrowth in her wake. She vaguely recalled the path she had taken on her horse through the trees — a horse she had never seen since. She supposed he had run free into the woods and never looked back.

With reckless hope, she trusted her instinct and led The Dwellings' most dangerous gang through the dense trees of Rundlewood Forest, imagining herself fleeing on horseback.

Where might she have run in her moment of panic? She followed her nose and hoped for the best.

The trees thinned ahead, and through the gaps in their trunks, she saw it at last. The archway stood crooked and unassuming in a clearing. Ebony froze. The forest felt suddenly too quiet, as if the wind itself were watching. Behind her, the Jades stumbled forward, laughing, jostling, blades drawn — but Ebony only stared at the arch. She had found the way back! Now she had to find the words.

"That's it?" the leader said quietly into her ear.

Ebony nodded, heart pounding. Unless they were very successfully hiding, there were no Foryx in sight. They either hadn't got her message or they had chosen to ignore her.

A prickle of panic climbed up her spine.

What now?

She had told herself she'd figure it out when she got here — that something would come to her, some spark of cunning or courage. But now, standing at the very threshold, her mind felt frighteningly blank.

Without the Fae and The Foryx, who was she? A girl in muddy boots, surrounded by a merciless gang, facing an ancient realm and a prophecy that would likely kill her.

"Well, Wick?" the leader snapped.

She strode up to the Fae Door with false purpose and knelt down before it, drawing the symbol for 'open' in the earthy ground. The Jades stood quiet behind her, anticipation murmuring through the trees. But nothing happened.

Her heart pounded so hard, she was sure every gang member there could hear it. Even the birds were listening and watching closely. Maybe the sign wasn't clear enough? She gathered some nearby sticks and laid them in the right shape. Still, nothing.

"You lied, Ebony Wick," the leader growled.

"No, I promise you—"

"You think we're fools, believing this old archway, this rubble, is some sort of entrance to a fairytale land! I'm not an idiot, Wick, I know a lie when I see one."

Ironically, that bit wasn't the lie.

A sharp kick landed in the back of her leg, and she stumbled to the floor and felt cold steel on her neck.

"I told you I would kill you myself," the leader growled.

"Please! I'm not lying! This is the Fae Door!"

"You will not humiliate me ever again, you filthy urchin," he spat.

Think, Ebony, think. Her heart thundered, drowning out every thought but fear. *They're going to kill you. This is it. She had to get the Fae's attention. But what would convince them to answer her call?*

She sucked in a breath, heart pounding so hard it hurt her ribs, and cried out, "King Alvero, please! I got rid of the mark! I am no longer marked by the Shadow!"

The name rang out across the clearing, raw and desperate, tearing from her like a last, defiant prayer.

"What?" the leader growled. "What are you on about?"

A gasp ran through the crowd behind them and the cold steel left Ebony's throat. She tentatively looked up to see a singular fairy buzzing furiously before her, staff at the ready. This was no dainty, colourful creature. It was in full battle mode, sharp and angular, a cruel expression on its face. Ebony's breath caught in her throat. The beauty of those little fairies she knew so well wasn't real. This was their true form. This was the creature that had murdered the Bounty Hunters. The creature she had thought she was in league with.

"They have come, Ebony Wick. The Shadows have come."

Ebony's stomach dropped out of her chest, leaving her hollow. The battle against the Shadows had already on the other side of the Fae Door. The Fae were fighting for their lives, and she had led the Jades here to distract them from the true fight.

Behind her, she could hear the Jades shifting, drawing blades, cursing under their breath, the leader growling out orders. *They still think they can win. They have no idea what's waiting for them.*

They needed rid of the Jades as soon as possible so they could focus on the true enemy.

"Kill them!" Ebony yelled at the fairy. "They are here to destroy you and the forest! Kill them! Kill them all!"

She scrambled to her feet and ran into the trees just as the screams started, but something tugged at her braid and pulled her back.

"Oh no you don't," a man growled into her ear and restrained her flailing arms. "You're going down with us."

If she died now, they'd never win the war against the Shadows. A new Daughter would be created, and the Fae would have no idea how to find her. But if she didn't die now, she and the Fae would have to fight the Shadows on their own. Would The Foryx answer her call after she had abandoned Sam to the Shadow?

Hunter was dead, and the Bounty Hunters decimated and disbanded. She had burned all of her bridges and lost any friends she had once had. And yet she, the Daughter of the Forest, was supposed to defeat the shadows and close the Shadow Door? They were all doomed. She had never been able to face *one* shadow, let alone them all!

Her body fell limp and she stopped struggling. It was no use. There was no point in trying to escape. Where would she go, anyway? No one would accept her. Even Rundlewood Forest was a dangerous place for her now, not a place of refuge. Her heartbeat slowed and she felt strangely calm in her defeat. She had spent so many years fighting for survival, and it had been exhausting. But it was all over now. She'd either be killed by The Jades or the Shadows. And there was nothing she could do about it.

The man holding her turned to face the fray, and Ebony's eyes grew wide. What had she done? What had she unleashed? Before her lay carnage. Flashes of light and singed flesh, burning men and women begging for relief. Begging to be killed. The Fae weren't killing them, they were torturing them, their sweet features twisted and sharp. And in that moment, Ebony hated them all. The Fae that had looked after her and stood by her side, that had let her into their inner sanctum. Scratch the surface and they were violent and cruel, and she had known that and still she had unleashed them on the Jades. Granted, they weren't much better. But who was the lesser of two evils?

The man's arms pinning her to his chest fell limp, and with a thud he fell to the floor behind her. The Fae had come for him.

Bu as she turned to look at him on the ground, she saw an arrow sticking out of his chest. The Fae hadn't killed him. So who had?

All around her through the trees, she began to see familiar faces emerge. For a breathless moment, Ebony thought her mind was playing tricks on her as, one by one, they stepped into view. Unwashed faces smudged with dirt and resolve, weapons raised and ready. The Foryx had arrived. Relief mixed with dread in Ebony's chest, her heart hammering so hard it hurt. Reinforcements — but at what cost? Were they all headed to their deaths?

But one face caught her attention — and it stopped Ebony's breath in her chest. Among the hard-eyed Foryx fighters stood the horrified, grief-stricken, and exhausted face of her aunt; a face covered in ash, with tearful streaks down her cheeks. Her fine clothes were singed at the hem, and strands of hair clung to her damp forehead.

Mary — here? Among The Foryx?

"STOP!" Ebony yelled. She ran into the fray. "Stop, Fae, stop!" She turned to The Foryx, their weapons raised and eyes full of fear. "Don't hurt the Fae!" She spun on her heel and bellowed at the top of her voice. "King Alvero, stop this violence! The Foryx will help in the war against the Shadows!" The woodland fell still and the screaming died down. She took a deep breath and glared at the Fae hovering around her. "The Shadow Door is open, and we need all the men we can get to beat the darkness. The Shadows won't care whose side you're on. They'll feed on all of us."

A swarm of light soared back through the Fae Door, blinking out as they disappeared, leaving the woods dark and quiet.

A solitary fairy flew towards Ebony. King Alvero, sharp and twisted, but unmistakably their king. "The Sister has been called. The Shadows have broken free. Our people are dying."

"It is time," Ebony said. "I have removed the Shadow's mark. I am ready to enter the Shadow Door and find the Mother."

She wasn't ready. She wasn't ready at all. But what did she have to lose?

King Alvero turned to face the army standing behind Ebony. "If you pledge to fight the shadows, then you are welcome in our realm."

Ebony's knees grew week and she collapsed to the floor. She had done it. She had put the prophecy in motion. The Daughter would open this door and somehow close another. She would help defeat the Shadows. But she had no idea how.

24

In the clearing before the archway, the air shimmered with something ancient and alive. The Fae King flew forward — fierce and otherworldly in his battle form. He raised his slender, claw-tipped hand towards the grim-faced Foryx and beckoned them towards him one by one. Mud-splattered and terrified, The Foryx and Southern Dwellers stepped up to the tiny yet intimidating king.

He touched their foreheads, causing a brief, searing sting of pain, causing them to flinch, gasp, or stagger back. And then, slowly, their hands began to glow, their veins like lightning up their forearms, and light pooled in their palms.

At first, they only stared at the light, half-fearful, half-awed. But soon, someone dared to test it: a young Foryx woman thrust out her palm, and a narrow spear of brilliance shot into the gloom. Murmurs rippled through the ranks; more hands rose, more lights flared to life. In the spaces between them, the damp forest seemed to brighten. This was how they would destroy the Shadows.

Yet Ebony felt the weight of what lay beyond the door — what they all must face. Even with this new power, the

Shadows were countless. Her blue ring shone on her finger, a reminder that she, too, carried a fragment of that same dangerous light, and she had wielded it long before the Fae had blessed the others. She had used it to shatter the Shadow that had haunted her for so long.

Across the clearing, the great archway pulsed with faint, beckoning blue. One at a time, The Foryx and Dwellers stepped through, vanishing into Faelynn and the war waiting there. Ebony swallowed, her heart thudding against bruised ribs.

An arm was wrapped around Ebony's shoulder, and she flinched.

"It's me, my dear. You're safe now." Her aunt's kind face smiled beside her, and Ebony launched into a hug.

"I'm not safe. Not at all. I've got to do the next bit now — close the Fae Door."

"I know. But half the prophecy has already taken place."

"What do you mean? It's hardly started."

"*With the Wick, unite the realms: the city, forest, and Fae,*" her aunt recited. How many times had she read her aunt's poem? "You've done that bit. The forest is The Foryx."

"But the city … The Jades were just wiped out. That's hardly uniting them."

"Not the Jades, my dear. I persuaded my people to help the cause. The Southern Dwellers."

"You— your underground movement?" Ebony looked around her and for the first time noticed that it wasn't just Foryx members surrounding her. Men and women wearing expensive silk robes strode past her, determination on their faces. The Southern Dwellings had risen up and joined them. "But how?"

Mary leaned in close and whispered, "I told them the Shadow had killed my husband."

Ebony raised her eyebrows. Mary's husband had died many moons ago and she had been keeping it a secret. Ebony hadn't realised he'd been so beloved, sparking enough loyalty for them to rise up against a dark and deadly force that none of them had ever met. That large and weaselly man she had once stolen from, Lord Donahue, had started a real movement.

"Thanks to you, the Jades shouldn't be a problem anymore," Mary added, "The Fae just wiped out most of them." She shivered.

"It was horrific."

"Oh and I believe another part of the prophecy has also

been put into motion. *Time draws near.* My aunt. Her name means 'time', remember? And the Fae said they have called her."

"But … now I have to close the door. I have no idea how."

"Did you know how to unite city, forest, and Fae?" Ebony shook her head, her eyes wide. It had all been quite a coincidence. "Exactly. You'll figure it out as you go along. Come on, now, I want to see what Faelynn is like after hearing so much about it."

She pulled Ebony back onto her feet and together, with trepidation, they entered the land of the Fae.

Ebony had expected the shining sun and perfect blue sky of the Fae realm; the luscious green grass and songbirds flitting over the ruined towers of the Mother's Abbey.

Instead, black clouds roiled overhead, boiling with flashes of white-blue lightning. The abbey itself was aflame — orange tongues of fire licking the stone walls, belching smoke into the churning sky.

All around them, the battle was already raging. Blasts of blinding light shot from outstretched palms; Fae and Foryx alike wielded that light like a blade, cutting through shadows that hissed and recoiled before disintegrating like shattered glass.

The screams of men and women echoed as the Shadows' clawed tendrils tore through them. Every touch from a Shadow warped minds. Many men could be seen rocking in corners, speaking in tongues. Dark shapes lunged and writhed at the edges of the firelight, barely glimpsed before they struck.

Rain hammered down, cold and heavy, slicking Ebony's hair to her neck. Thunder cracked overhead, shaking the ground beneath her boots.

She instinctively leapt to one side as a wall of darkness swept past her, tendrils trailing behind it like a cloak. A bolt of Fae lightning slammed into it mid-air, splintering it into nothingness. Heart pounding, Ebony stumbled forward, nearly tripping over a fallen Dweller whose chest no longer rose.

She steadied herself, breath ragged, and raised her trembling hand. The silver ring on her finger shimmered, its sapphire stone flaring with a bright, defiant blue. Shadows coiled toward her, drawn by her fear.

With a cry torn from her throat, Ebony thrust her hand forward, and a beam of brilliant blue light erupted from the ring, slicing through the darkness. The nearest Shadow shrieked as the light tore through its smoky form, its red eyes flaring wide before it disappeared.

Her own eyes burned, glowing red as blood, the same red as the eyes of the creatures she fought — yet hers blazed with something different: fury, desperation, resolve. Another Shadow lunged; Ebony spun, ducking low, and sent another burst of light spearing through its centre. It shuddered, writhed, then fell apart like smouldering paper.

For a breathless moment, she stood among the drifting ashes, chest heaving, rain soaking her hair and shoulders, ring still glowing in her clenched fist. All around her, the night screamed and burned — and Ebony Wick stood at its heart, refusing to run.

Through the smoke and panic emerged two familiar faces: a man hanging off the shoulder of a young woman, his face sickly, his skin grey.

"Daya!" Ebony cried and ran towards her. "Sam?" Her voice trembled. She gave Daya a worried and questioning expression.

"It seems I joined The Foryx just after you left them," Daya called back, her voice raw from shouting over the chaos. "Sam is … well …" She frowned.

"Admit it," he croaked. "I'm dying."

He looked at Ebony and tried to smile, but was thin,

guarded. It wasn't the loving, friendly smile she had got to know. A lot had happened to them both since she had gone. Since she had abandoned him. Lightning flashed, revealing the haunted look in his eyes.

"I'll leave you two to talk," Daya said, lowering Sam carefully to the wet grass before turning away.

"Daya," Ebony called after her. "It's so good to see you."

"Is it?" she shot back and strode away.

Ebony took a deep breath and looked down at Sam, who was waiting expectantly. All around, shadows shrieked, Fae lightning danced across the field, and dying men groaned.

"Mary!" Ebony looked around desperately, but her aunt was nowhere to be seen. She was gone — lost among firelit silhouettes.

Ebony forced herself to look Sam in the eye as she dropped to her knees beside him, ignoring the rainwater soaking through her trousers.

"I abandoned you to the Shadow. I chose myself over my closest friend and I will never forgive myself for that."

He gave a weak shrug. "Given your history with the Shadow, I think anyone would have done the same. Besides,

I didn't tell you the full extent of it — how much control it had over me."

"Had?" she echoed. "So it doesn't anymore?"

"Took my life force and left me. But without it, I'm withering away. I should have died that day it rescued me. It has kept me standing, and now time is catching up to me."

"Why are you here then? You should be resting!"

"I'm *dying*, Ebony. There's nothing I can do about it, and hell if I'm going to sit by and watch my friends die at the hands of the shadows."

She swallowed heavily. "You're a better person than me."

"You're here, aren't you? You warned us and told us what to do, where to go."

She opened her mouth, hesitated, rain dripping from her chin. "I feel like I don't have a choice," she confessed. "The prophecy says—"

"Prophecy?"

"Yep. I'm in a prophecy. The Daughter, Mother, and Sister of the Forest have to unite to destroy the Shadow. I'm the Daughter."

Sam gave her a look of confusion then gave a bark of laughter. "A Fae thing, I assume?"

She managed the smallest smile, despite the horror around them. Nearby, a Dweller unleashed a beam of light that vaporised a lunging shadow mid-leap. She hadn't expected anyone else to understand, and she suddenly felt very grateful that her aunt knew everything. No more secrets.

She got to her feet, leaving Sam doing all he could from the floor with his newfound light. A hulking Dweller to her left roared as he swung his beam of light through a swarm of shadows, the blue-white glare splitting the darkness apart. Ebony ducked behind him, letting his bulk shield her, then darted forward to drive her own beam into a shadow slipping past his guard. Smoke exploded around them, acrid and bitter in her lungs.

Around her, the Southern Dwellers surged forward, faces set with grim determination. Men and women she had once seen as enemies now fought beside her, palms glowing with borrowed Faelight.

To her right, a young woman with a scar across her jaw locked eyes with Ebony for a heartbeat, and together they turned their beams on another advancing shadow. It withered and collapsed into nothing between them. The woman nodded once — a silent truce forged in the heat of battle — and Ebony nodded back, heart hammering.

The storm howled overhead, and the burning abbey bathed the clearing in a restless, hellish glow. Shards of ruined stone lay underfoot, slick with rain and ash. More shadows spilled from the cracked door, writhing across the grass, but the Southern Dwellers, The Foryx, the Fae, and Ebony met them head-on.

Every pulse of her blue ring was a promise: she was here, she was fighting, and she would not run again.

A cold chill prickled her spine. The familiar pull of the Shadow Door made her turn toward it, dark mist bleeding from the archway, curling over the grass and covering the field.

Lightning split the sky above the abbey ruins, throwing the door into sharp relief. A jagged crack could be seen across its dark, rippling surface.

"It is time, Wick," King Alvero said, standing on her shoulder. "The Dwellings are lost unless someone crosses into the Shadow realm and closes the door. It is time."

A swarm of Fae surrounded her, lighting her figure like a beacon, and when they left her and rejoined the battle, Ebony inspected the marks they had made on her body with the staining berry juice. They'd used this on her once before, the night before she had been banished.

Every bit of skin showing was now covered in red marks: Fae symbols. She recognised some of them: courage, sight, strength of mind, and, most importantly, 'open'; the same symbol repeated all over her, ready to help her open the Shadow Door and let her enter: a line through a cross.

Ebony's heart thundered. She wiped rain and sweat from her brow, the storm raging around her. Shadows screamed in the dark, and she could barely hear her own thoughts over the roar of wind and battle.

She took one shaky breath, her boots sinking into bloodied mud, and stepped forward.

25

Her heart pounding in her chest, Ebony stopped walking as she heard Sam's distinctive voice, crying out with pain from somewhere across the field.

She turned to look at the carnage. Beautiful Faelynn, now a blackening, fiery, pit of despair — exactly what the Shadows wanted. She turned back to the black door, gathering her courage to enter the Shadowlands.

Mist seeped from the shimmering door and grew thicker, and before her a figure formed. A figure with red eyes and willowy tendrils.

"Go, Ebony! Go!" Sam cried from across the field.

Ebony stood in the centre of a storm of light, a silent battle. Rain began to pour as streams of the Fae's light shot through the shadows, breaking them apart piece by piece, but more and more shadows took their place, slashing, slicing through flesh like it was paper. Her ring shone a bright blue from her hand, protecting her like a bubble of light. The shadows feared that light. She would be safe on the other side of the door.

She took a few tentative steps towards the black archway and stepped through.

Ash clung to her hair like frost as she emerged in the blackened world of the Shadow realm. The forest vanished behind her, swallowed by the thick, humming dark. A stillness pressed on her chest. The world around her had a blue tinge, her ring lighting the path before her. Ahead, the burnt city sprawled just as it had in her dreams: towers collapsed in jagged heaps, streets cracked and carpeted with ash. But it wasn't just a dream this time. She was here now — in the flesh. She no longer saw shadows in the burning streets. All was quiet. The shadows were out and decimating her friends.

She looked back at the archway and could see the same crack on this side. What had stopped the Mother being able to get back through? If someone as powerful as her had been trapped … how was Ebony going to get back? She couldn't think about that now. She just had to find a way to close the door. And all she could think to do was find the Mother. *She* must know how to do it. A small part of Ebony was aware that if the Mother knew how to do it, she would have done so by now, having been trapped here all these years. Another thing she couldn't think about right now.

She began the familiar walk through the blackened streets, her boots wading through ash, and the deeper she went, the more the air hummed — not with noise, but with intent. With *wanting*. The dark will of the shadows permeated every pore of this blackened city.

"Where are you?" Ebony called, her voice trembling against the silence.

The answer was a long exhale behind her.

She spun.

Nothing.

"I need to speak to you. I know you're here somewhere," she said to nothing and no one.

She continued walking through the city, smoke rising from the very cobbles she trod on. The place was almost *made* from ash and smoke. The silence was so deafening, even her own breath made her jump. Desperate to see the Mother's golden hair, she started to imagine it — a flicker of colour disappearing around a corner, then a flash of gold from a tall tower.

"Where are you?" she called into the darkness. "They're all gone! All the shadows are in Faelynn. Everything you built is being torn to shreds and burnt to ashes, just like this place. I need your help!"

"You are The Child of the Line. You should not have come here."

Ebony jumped and spun around. Behind her stood a tall, thin woman with long, blonde hair and sharp blue eyes. She was ethereal and intimidating, yet soft, with a kind face.

"I need to close the door," Ebony said. "Fully. Properly. The cracks are letting them through — all of them. But …"

"You don't know how."

Ebony nodded. "I thought—"

"You thought I might know how to close the door, so you came looking for me. You should not have come."

"Why not? Won't you help me?"

"I never closed it."

Ebony's heart sank. This was exactly what she had dreaded. "But you must have had a plan when you came through the Shadow Door. You must have had some idea of what to do."

"My power …"

"You could speak to the dead, right?"

The Mother nodded. "But it changed. I could do *more* … It wasn't safe." She turned and began walking away.

"Wait!" Ebony caught up with her and walked alongside her through the burning streets.

"I cannot help you. I cannot leave this place."

"What do you mean? Why?"

"I *sealed* the door, Ebony. I didn't close it fully. The only way to close it fully is to unite the Mother, Sister, and Daughter of the Forest. Together, our power can shut them out for good."

Ebony beamed. The poem had alluded to that, and the Mother clearly knew what to do once they were all united.

"The Sister is on the way! I'm the Daughter, and I've found you now. So what are we waiting for?"

"I cannot go back!" The Mother stopped in her tracks and looked Ebony dead in the eye. "My powers changed. I couldn't just *speak* to the dead, I could bring them back, Ebony. I could resurrect those we had lost over the years. And I did. I pulled them from their realm of peace for my own selfish gain, and it blackened them. A shadow was cast over them. They became less and less human every day, see-through, like smoke. Their eyes turned red, their souls dark. They wanted control. They wanted the world to suffer like the twisted thoughts in their minds made them suffer. Ebony,

I *made* the shadows." She gave Ebony a guilty look. "I expect the Fae told you the darkness came to Faelynn through the outside world, that the world demanded balance and with balance came darkness."

Ebony nodded, her brow creased. Had they not told her the truth?

"I let them believe that. But after creating the first Shadow, the Shadow Door appeared in Faelynn. By selfishly bringing my loved ones back from the dead, darkness found them, and a colony of shadows was born, created from the first — the one that has haunted you and the Three. They began taking more of our loved ones, seeping away their life-force, coercing them into the Shadowlands. So you see? I can't go back."

"Well, you can't change what you did. It's too late now, and the shadows are winning. If you come back, you can redeem yourself, fight them off, end them for good."

"You don't understand. The first Shadow took my mind and I couldn't stop. More and more shadows were created until their darkness overtook Faelynn and they were uncontrollable. The Fae, the Sister, and the Daughter had to work together to open the door to the Shadow realm. I convinced them to … I told them I'd be able to find a way to close it from the inside …" The Mother gave her a look that said everything she dared not voice.

"You didn't have a way, did you? You stepped through the Shadow Door and never looked back."

"I knew how to seal it from the inside … but closing it forever meant I'd have to stay in Faelynn, forever creating more shadows. I was a danger to the world. I *am* a danger. If I go to the surface, the Shadow will take me again and it will win."

"It's winning anyway," Ebony said darkly. "We have an army fighting them, but they won't win if we don't do something soon. They will get through the Fae Door and they will take The Dwellings, and who knows what then?"

The Mother slowly shook her head. "You don't understand …"

"I do! The Shadow creates fear. It makes you want to run, flee, and never look back. I have done the same my whole life. I have run from everything and everyone and all it does it cause more death and destruction. If I can face the shadows, a lowly urchin with no parents, then the Mother can too. This is the prophecy. The Mother, the Sister, and the Daughter must unite. *Will* unite. Now, come on! We have to leave this place."

She went to grab the Mother's wrist, but her hand passed right through her.

"I am becoming shadow."

"You've been in this awful place too long. You need Faelynn and it needs you. And I will find a way to get you back through that damn door even if it kills me. I'm not abandoning them again. Sam needs me."

The Mother smiled. "You have changed, Ebony Wick. I no longer sense fear in you." She sighed. "If I come with you, I will die. I am too old for the mortal realm."

Ebony took a deep breath. "You're dying here anyway. You're becoming one of *them*."

The Mother nodded sadly. "Perhaps it is my time to die."

"And in doing so, you will save so many people and you will pass on the title of the Mother, and the Three can always be united to keep the Shadow Door closed." She understood now. The door had been weak all these years because the Three couldn't be united, and that was why she had been drawn to this place in her dreams. She had been subconsciously seeking the Mother all this time.

"Strangely enough, I will miss this place … it is so quiet," the Mother said, almost to herself.

"So you're coming?"

"Yes, Ebony Wick. I am coming. It is time to say goodbye."

The pair, one with shining hair, the other with shining eyes, walked back through the streets and towards the cracked Shadow Door. The Mother took one last look back and stepped forward. Ebony followed.

26

They stepped through the arch and into ruin. Faelynn was unrecognisable. The forest was scorched, the trees' bark blackened and smouldering. Ash rained like snow. Fires crackled through the abbey, bodies littered the wet ground, and the air was thick with screams — not Dweller, not Fae, but something older and breaking. The people were fighting back, but the shadows were winning.

Above, the moon bled down pale light, struggling to hold its shape. Shadows spilled through the trees like oil, consuming everything they touched, and everywhere lay scattered and broken bodies, Dweller, Foryx, and Fae alike. Ebony had never seen a dead fairy before. They had always seemed invincible. But there they lay, in their innocent form, strewn on the ground like large flies, their delicate, shining wings still and splayed on the grass.

The Mother took in the scene, her face unreadable. But Ebony staggered forward, heart pounding. Too late. She had come back too late.

And then — from across the battlefield, through smoke and ruin — a figure stepped forward. A woman, tall and unflinching, with a wild mane of white, curly hair. Her cloak was torn, her eyes fierce.

Ebony gasped.

A warmth bloomed in her chest, and something ancient clicked into place. She didn't understand it, didn't need to.

She *knew*.

The Three were here.

Ebony's legs moved without command. The other two women did the same. They stepped across the battlefield, drawn together not by reason or instinct, but by something older.

They didn't speak.

Didn't plan.

Just walked.

And when they met, a sound reverberated around them, like a breath drawn in by the universe.

Then light exploded.

It poured from their feet, their chests, their mouths — it cracked the air, shattered the sky. It rolled outward like a tidal wave. Every shadow it touched burned into nothingness, dissolved without sound or struggle. The smoke vanished. The black ash turned to white.

And in the centre of it all: the Shadow Door.

It screamed — not with sound, but with *ending*. The crack split wide, then shattered like glass. A thousand shards of darkness splintered into the sky, then blinked out like stars dying.

Gone.

The light faded.

The sky turned blue.

And the birds began to sing again.

The Mother looked at Ebony one last time. She smiled — not with joy, but with peace. Her body wavered, her edges growing soft, as if she were becoming mist, memory.

Then she was gone.

A wisp. A sigh. A soul returning to rest.

Faelynn had returned to its endless, endless summer, but bodies and decay still lay strewn all about the place. Ebony and Tessara collapsed to the floor and the world went black.

When she awoke, Ebony found Tessara on the ground beside her, breathing heavily and shielding her eyes against the blue sky.

"She's gone, isn't she?" Tessara asked. "The Mother."

"She knew she would die when she returned. But in her place—"

"Somewhere right now a new Mother is being born at long last. The line will continue." They both sat upright, and Tessara held Ebony's hand in hers.

"The Shadow Door will never form again," Ebony said. "The door to that realm cannot open … unless …"

"Unless what?"

"Well, the Mother created the Shadows by accident … by resurrecting the dead."

The Sister's eyes widened, mouth parting in horror. For a heartbeat she looked as though she might speak, but no words came — just the shock settling on her face, her gaze turning inward as if reworking all she knew about the Three and the history of the Shadows.

"If the new Mother can do the same …" Ebony shook her head slowly.

"The power of the line diminishes with each new birth. We'll just have to hope the new Mother doesn't have that power … or doesn't work out that she has it."

"Maybe we should find her?"

The Sister shrugged. "We have time. She's not even born yet, and then it could take years for her to find her power, if she ever does."

Ebony smiled with relief. "We did it. We closed the door and defeated the shadows!"

"*You* did it. You worked out how to do it. You united all these people."

"I have no idea how, even now!" Ebony laughed.

"But you did the impossible."

Ebony blew out a breath, a weight falling from her shoulders, and then it hit her. She knew what she wanted to do now. Where she wanted to go.

"I have nowhere to go, Tess. I have no home. Mary's house burned down. And I definitely don't want to stay here …"

Ebony had loved Faelynn it once. Now it just irritated her. No sense of time passing was disorienting. And too much had happened between her and the Fae. She couldn't feel safe or peaceful around them, knowing what they were capable of.

"You need a fresh start. You need to leave The Dwellings. Come to Henley. Live with me. Start anew."

She had been hoping to hear those words, and suddenly

the world came into focus and Ebony began to notice the noise around her. Tears, exhaustion, laughter, chatter … a woman's voice ordering people around. Before them loomed the ruins of the Mother's Abbey, now swarming with men and women, hundreds of Fae flitting about amongst them, the large tree still standing proudly before them. Ebony could swear it was bigger than before.

"See to your friends, Ebony, then we will go home. I'll speak to your aunt and give her any help she might need."

Ebony smiled and clambered to her feet, a sense of peace soaring through her every fibre, a calm she had never felt before. She strode towards Daya, who was sitting in the grass a hundred yards away.

"What happened, Ebony? No one really understands …"

"The Three united," Ebony replied cryptically, sitting down next to her. "I know it doesn't make any sense, but the Mother, Sister, and Daughter of the Forest united and … I don't know exactly. We banished the darkness."

"None of that made a lick of sense."

"I'll explain it to you one day. Where's Sam?"

Daya shook her head slowly and frowned. "Sam …"

Ebony sighed. "His body drifted away like mist in the wind?"

Daya gawped. "How did you know?"

"The same thing happened to the Mother. The Shadow took his life force. But he's at peace now. I'm just sad I didn't get to say goodbye."

"You were doing more important things."

Ebony looked around at Faelynn, buzzing with activity, a mixture of Southerners, Foryx, and Fae, all helping each other like comrades. The Jades were defeated, thanks to the Fae, and Mary seemed to be negotiating with Foryx members. She caught Ebony's eye and beamed.

"I'm going now, Daya," Ebony said. "I'm leaving The Dwellings. I might see you again one day."

Daya nodded. "I figured as much. You never quite fit in."

Ebony laughed and got to her feet before walking towards the outstretched arms of her aunt.

"You did it! I knew you would! You Three are still as magic as ever."

"But so many died …"

"Yes," Mary said sadly. "But so many have been saved."

"Where are you going to go now? Your house …"

"I have friends who can put me up for the time being.

I'll find a new house. I need to be in The Dwellings, to forge its future without Snatchers or Jades. It's an exciting time."

"Just … make it equal, okay? The Commoners and the North Dwellings …"

"We will. But where will you go? I can't promise my friends will be happy to house the girl with red eyes who just lit up the night and destroyed the deadliest things they've ever seen. I think we're all a bit scared of you."

Great. More looks of fear everywhere she went. Another reason to leave this place.

"I'm going to live in Henley with Tess."

Mary nodded with a smile. "I'll visit you as often as I can, my dear. It looks like my aunt is ready for you."

At the entrance to the Fae realm, Tessara stood looking at Ebony across the field. Ebony hugged her aunt and made her way back to the Fae Door, where King Alvero and Queen Coralia hovered by the Sister.

"Goodbye, Wick. You are in good hands."

Ebony wanted to look on the Fae with fondness, and almost expected a sad goodbye, but instead all she felt was bitter and angry. They were violent, cruel, ruthless. Everything she never wanted to be. She was glad to be rid of them and their cryptic ways.

"I won't be coming back here," she said firmly, and King Alvero nodded.

Ebony took one last look before decidedly stepping through the Fae Door.

On the other side, survivors had begun to make their way home through the trees, trampling pathways through the undergrowth. To the right stood a coach and two impatient horses, ready to take Ebony and Tessara to Henley.

Epilogue

Henley was the kind of town that made you forget there had ever been death, or shadows, or fear.

The hedgerows were turning rust-red and gold, and chimney smoke curled into the pale morning sky as they arrived in Tessara's rickety old coach. Ebony was glad to be free of it and stretched her aching muscles after climbing out. Someone nearby was baking — cinnamon, maybe, or nutmeg. The scent drifted between houses and made the air feel warm, even as the season turned crisp.

"I'm going for a walk. Be back soon," she announced. Perhaps she should have said 'be *home* soon'? It was, after all, her home now. And something deep inside told her this was her forever home. No survival, fear, or anger here. Just a new world; a new start.

Ebony walked with her hands deep in her pockets, the sleeves of her borrowed coat rolled twice at the wrists. Leaves crackled underfoot. She didn't know where she was walking. She just followed the quiet stillness through the peaceful town.

Down a narrow lane, a low stone wall lined one side of

the path, on the other side of which was a lovely front garden — well kept, but natural; not the box hedges of the South Dwellings.

And then she saw him.

He was kneeling beside a row of dark soil, tucking bulbs into the earth with his bare hands. His coat lay discarded nearby, and there was dirt on his cheek. A small basket of root vegetables sat by his knee. He looked older. Or maybe just lighter.

Ebony's breath caught in her throat.

"Hicks?" she said. "Is that you?"

The man looked up, blinking into the sun — and when he saw her, a slow, disbelieving smile spread across his face.

"Ebony," he said, barely louder than a breath. "What are you doing here?"

"This is my home now." She pointed roughly in the direction of Tessara's house.

He glanced past her, then back. "Henley's not going to know what hit it."

Ebony laughed, the sound catching somewhere between her chest and her throat. She crossed the garden without thinking, boots sinking into soft ground, and wrapped her arms around him. He smelled like earth and woodsmoke. She hadn't realised how much she'd missed him.

The door had closed. The shadows were gone. She had made it through.

And at last — at long last — she was home.

Places that inspired this trilogy

If you want to discover and visit the places that inspired the Dwelling Hunter series, see below for more information.

Rundlewood Forest
Inspired by the woodland I grew up very close to. I would happily lose myself in the trees and then find my way back to the main paths.
Place: Laughton Common Wood, Laughton, East Sussex
What3words: eyelashes.departure.hurtles

Faelynn
When I lived in Guildford (Surrey, UK), we frequented the ruins of a spectacular abbey. The yew tree here directly inspired the Fae's tree in Faelynn and the abbey inspired the Mother's Abbey. This abbey was also used in the filming of *Into the Woods*, for some with the actress Meryl Streep.
Place: Waverly Abbey, Farnham, Surrey
What3words: scared.hawks.cloak

The surrounding fields around the Mother's Abbey were inspired by an old abbey ruin on the Norfolk Broads.
Place: St Benet's Abbey, Horning, Norfolk

What3words: heartened.kind.themes

The Fae Door and The Shadow Door

Inspired by a ruined church buried in the woods. Here there are archways standing alone — no walls either side of them. The temptation to walk through the archways is strong! Though they definitely feel otherworldly.

Place: Mannington Church, Itteringham (ruins)

What3words: performed.warthog.ideas

MADDY GLENN grew up inspired by the rolling Sussex countryside, which sparked her love of storytelling. Following a degree in Philosophy and English Literature, she established Softwood Books, now a multiple award-winning publisher for independent authors. Maddy is a published poet and the author of *The Dwelling Hunter* fantasy series, *On the Edge* (2020), *In the Dark* (2022), and *At the Door* (2025). She lives in rural Suffolk with her family.

Instagram: @maddyglenn
Author Photograph: Penny Morgan